THE FACEOFF

WYNCOTE WOLVES
BOOK FOUR

CALI MELLE

Cover Designer: Cat Imb, TRC Designs

Editor: Rumi Khan

To whoever said don't hate the player, hate the game...
You had it wrong all along.
You can hate both and still get a good orgasm out of it.

PROLOGUE

HAYDEN

Standing by the fire with Sterling and Simon, I slowly sip my beer as they both talk about our hockey game from earlier. It's the summer, so some of the guys went back home to spend the time off from school with their families. A few of us stayed back, since we've laid our roots in the small town in Vermont after coming here to play for Wyncote.

The guys who stayed back are all in the summer hockey league to keep up with the demands of meeting our main goal—playing professionally after graduation. In the fall, most of us will be starting our senior year, so we have to stay focused on what we really came here for. The education is above average, but the hockey program at Wyncote is where you want to be.

After my fuckup last year, coming here was the best move I could have made. Although I came halfway through the season, I ended up fitting in well with the team and making my place known. I'm exactly where I belong and it helps having three of my childhood friends along my side.

Although, the three of them are practically wifed up now, so you won't see them hanging out at a party like this. Sterling and Simon insisted that I come to the party that Derrick was throwing at the lake. And they were right when they said that it was going to be a rager.

Tuning the two of them out, I see a girl standing across the fire, her eyes narrowed on me. Tilting my head to the side, I raise an eyebrow at her suspiciously. I don't recall ever seeing her anywhere before because she has the type of face that is impossible to erase from your memory.

Staring at her through the flames, my eyes travel across her perfectly symmetrical face. I can't see her eyes clearly, but through the smoke, they look like golden honey. Her hair hangs in perfect waves of amber down to her waist. She shifts her weight on her feet and my eyes trail down her slim torso and long legs.

The summers in Vermont get warm and her t-shirt and shorts hug the curves of her body perfectly. She stares back at me with a curious look before looking to the girl beside her as they fall into a conversation. She's a mystery to me and I need to shake the warmth that spreads through my body. I like to indulge in distractions from time to time, but she doesn't look like the type that would just be that.

I drain the rest of my beer before leaving the guys at the fire as I head over to the keg. As I fill up my plastic cup, I chug the light-colored liquid before filling it up again. Those light brown eyes drift into my mind and I know I need to erase them. Especially when she looks like she's fallen from heaven herself.

"You good, man?" Simon asks me as he comes up beside me and fills up his cup too. His eyes are on mine, his eyebrows drawn together in confusion as he watches me chug my beer again.

I nod, wiping the liquid from my mouth with the back of my hand, before holding my cup to him to refill it. "The heat from the fire was getting to me." And the heated gaze from the other side of the flames.

"I would tell you to go jump in the lake, but maybe not, considering how much you've drank already."

A chuckle vibrates through my chest and I lightly punch him in the arm. "I'm good, bro, but thanks for looking out for me."

"Sure," he smiles back at me as some girl comes up to him, sliding her arm through his. Simon glances down at her before looking back to me as she tugs on him. "I'll catch up with you later."

Nodding at him, I watch as he walks away with the girl. My eyes scan the shore of the lake, noticing that Sterling's sitting at the fire with some girl on his lap. I'm not surprised, seeing both of them hooking up with some random chicks. Since that seems to be what we do on the regular, unlike August, Logan, and Cam. They all ended up in the relationships that we've been trying to avoid.

Stepping away from the keg, I noticed that the golden-eyed beauty disappeared. And I don't feel like standing around while Sterling swallows some chick's tongue. Turning my back to them, I head toward the lake, stepping onto the wooden dock as I make my way down to the end of it. The sides are lined with lights and the sound of the water eases my soul as I sit down along the edge.

Hanging my arms over the railing, I sip my beer as I stare out at the dark water, the sounds from the party behind me. Music plays from the speakers set up on the beach, but it doesn't drown out the rippling sounds of the lake against the dock.

"You know, the party is back there," a soft, singsong voice wraps itself around my eardrums. The sound is like silk, like a melody that I could get lost in. A shiver rises up my spine as I crane my neck, glancing over my shoulder.

The girl from earlier steps closer to me, not stopping until she drops down on the dock beside me. "I don't blame you for coming out here. It's peaceful by the water... although, you strike me as someone who would prefer chaos instead."

Turning my head to look at her, I raise an eyebrow at her. "Do I know you?"

Her brown eyes are brighter than they appeared at the fire and the ghost of a smile plays on her lips. "Not yet."

My eyes widen slightly, a smirk forming on my face as I stare back at her. She's a goddamn mystery and now she has my fucking attention.

"What's your name?" I ask her, my voice thick with tension as my cock grows in my pants. I can't help myself as the scent of her perfume—a light vanilla smell—invades my senses.

She shakes her head at me. "I'm not here to exchange names or numbers with you. I'm here because I need a distraction and you looked like the perfect candidate for a bad decision when I saw you across the fire."

"What do you need a distraction from, pretty girl?" I question her, tilting my head to the side in curiosity. The alcohol is heavy in my system now and I'd be lying if I said that I wasn't drunk. Judging by the glossiness in her gaze, I think she's close to the same level as me.

"Hard pass," she laughs lightly, the sound vibrating against my eardrums. "I'm not here to divulge any of my secrets. I told you what I'm here for."

"You want me to be your bad decision?" My lips curl upward into a sinister smirk as I rise to my feet and extend my hand to her. "I can be whatever you want me to be, baby."

She slides her palm against mine, the warmth spreading up my arm like liquid fire as she wraps her slender fingers around my hand. I pull her to her feet and she stands up in front of me. Tilting my head down, I notice that even though she's got legs for days, she's still a good six inches shorter than me.

Her eyes shine up at me under the moonlight, bouncing back and forth between mine as she narrows them at me. "Before you start on some gentleman shit, yes, I am drunk and, yes, I am still sure."

Reaching out to her, I brush a piece of hair away from her face and tuck it behind her ear. Her lips part slightly as I drag my fingertips down the length of her throat, feeling her soft skin shiver under my touch. Dropping my face to hers, my lips lightly brush against hers, our breaths mixing together.

"Don't worry, baby. I'm not a gentleman."

"Good," she breathes, her voice husky as she laces her fingers through mine. "Come with me."

I let her lead me down the dock, back toward the party. As our feet reach the beach, she begins to walk in the opposite direction, taking me with her as we walk through the sand. This isn't the first time that I've had a girl approach me like this. And who am I to say no? I don't have any commitments holding me back.

"Where are we going?" I question her, as she leads me toward a clearing the leads through the trees.

She glances over her shoulder at me, mischief dancing in her eyes. "You'll see."

As we walk through the clearing, she leads me down a path to where there's at least a dozen tents set up. I stop in my tracks, confused by the scene laid out in front of me, when it clicks in my drunken mind. Sterling had mentioned that some people were camping here, just so they didn't have to worry about drinking and driving. I kind of tuned him out when he said that, because I wasn't the one driving here and finding a place to crash was never hard for me.

She leads me past a few of the tents before she stops by one that's tucked away in the far corner. "This one is mine," she whispers as she unzips the door to the tent and steps inside, pulling me in with her. It's hard to see in the darkness of the night and I trip over something that feels like a duffle bag.

There's an air mattress lying in the center with an open sleeping bag on top of it. I watch her, my heart pounding in my chest as she slowly spins around to face me, her hand leaving mine. We stand in silence for a moment, our breathing shallow as our eyes adjust to how we look in the dark. Stepping toward her, my hands reach out for her hips and I jerk her toward me until her body is crashing into mine.

"You sure you want this, babe?" I question her, sliding my hand along the back of her neck as she tilts her head back to look up at me.

"You ask a lot of questions for someone with a playboy reputation, King," she murmurs, my last name rolling off her tongue like that's exactly where it belongs.

And I want to fucking taste it.

———

EDEN

Hayden King.

One of the hockey team's biggest playboys. He came to Wyncote halfway through the year last year and he has quite the reputation already. Rumor has it, he slept with his coach's daughter at the last school he was at and got himself into some trouble when she wanted more from him. From what I was told, his parents were able to get him transferred quietly.

Nothing happens quietly, though, does it?

People always talk and someone will always find out about your deepest, darkest secret.

And what I'm about to do with Hayden is going to be mine.

I didn't like him from the moment I met him. He's cocky and arrogant, and it doesn't help that most people treat him like he walks on water. He fits in well with the hockey team and since he's a great addition to their roster, it makes him even more liked.

By everyone except me...

I'm not surprised that Hayden doesn't know who I am. Even though he's seen me at the ice rink numerous times, his head is always too far up his own ass to realize anything that's going on around him. I've avoided him like the plague until this very moment.

I need something to distract me from life and Hayden King is the perfect candidate. He is the worst possible decision that I could make right now and he's never looked better. I'm not blind, I know how attractive he is. I've just refused to be another notch in his belt until tonight. But this is happening on my terms.

Hayden is just along for the ride—to play the

part of the guy that I'll regret sleeping with in the morning.

His face dips down to mine, his lips colliding with mine as he dives his hand into my hair. Wrapping my arms around the back of his neck, our bodies are pressed flush against one another as he devours me, swallowing me whole. His mouth moves with mine, claiming me as his in this moment. Too bad it's just in this moment and that I hate him in real life.

I feel his tongue as it slides along the seam of my lips, slowly pushing them open as he wants more. Parting my lips, I let him in. His tongue slides against mine and his mouth is warm. He tastes like the alcohol he was drinking. He tastes like a bad decision and that's exactly why he's in my tent right now.

Hayden's fingers tangle in my hair, his tongue is in my mouth and I can't think straight with him this close. The smell of his cologne penetrates my nose and I inhale the scent, memorizing everything about him and this moment. Just because we're enemies doesn't mean that I can't store this in my brain for another time.

After the nasty breakup that I had freshman year, I swore off hockey players altogether. I ended up in over my head, deep in a serious relationship with the star player on the team who was a senior. We hit it off from the start, given that I'm a figure skater and we both practically lived on the ice. I believed every damn promise he made me while we were together, only to have him drop me the minute he graduated and got drafted into the NHL.

It made things awkward between the rest of the hockey team and myself. How could I continue being friends with any of the guys that I grew close to during that relationship I was in? I was left with no choice but to distance myself from them entirely. They were no longer my friends and because of that, Hayden was deemed my enemy by association.

He's the exact type of person that I've been trying to avoid since I had my heart shattered into a million pieces.

Hayden presses his hips against me, distracting me from my thoughts. Given our height difference, I can feel his cock pressing against my stomach through his pants. A moan slips from my lips as he tugs on my hair and he swallows the sound whole. My head swims as he drains the oxygen from my lungs, kissing me like I've never been kissed before.

Abruptly breaking apart, Hayden drops his mouth to my neck, burying his face as he nips at my skin. My heart pounds erratically in its cage as I inhale as much oxygen that my lungs will allow. His kiss leaves me dizzy, my knees feeling weak as a warmth spreads through the pit of my stomach. Sure, I can still feel the alcohol that I drank earlier, but this is something completely different now.

I'm clearheaded enough to know what I'm doing.

And everything between us is driven purely from lust and need.

Hayden drops his hands from my head and I cling onto him as I feel his touch trailing down my torso. His lips are still against my neck, licking and tasting every inch of skin he can find. Fingertips graze my waist as he slides them under the bottom hem of my shirt. It isn't long before he's pushing it up my body, my arms breaking away from him as he lifts my shirt over my head.

It's dark in here, but the light from the small camping area illuminates part of the tent. I can't see Hayden's face completely, but I can see his shadow as he moves in front of me. He drops my shirt onto the floor beside us, his lips finding my collarbone as he unclasps my bra and peels it from my body. I pay no mind as he discards it and his mouth finds my breast.

My knees feel like they're going to buckle under his touch as he continues his slow assault on my nipple. Hayden slides an arm around my back, holding me upright as he sucks and nips at my pebbled skin. His tongue swirls around it, flicking back and forth before he abruptly pulls away. The feeling of his breath causes a shiver to tear up my spine as he lightly blows on my damp skin.

Hayden moves his mouth to my other breast, repeating the same action as he continues to hold me upright. I feel like I could come undone, just from him playing with my nipples. Clamping my thighs together, I search for some type of friction or relief. My pussy is literally throbbing, just begging to be touched by him like the rest of my body.

Grabbing his shoulders, I push him away. Hayden stumbles back, but quickly regains his footing, stepping back into my space. He tilts his head as he looks down at me. "Something wrong, baby?"

"If clothes are coming off, I'm not the only one who's being stripped down."

Hayden turns his head slightly, a sliver of light hitting his face as a smirk plays on his lips. I don't miss the sinister mischief dancing in his irises as he stares back at me. "I told you that I'll be whatever you want, but if you want me to be naked, I want you taking my clothes off."

Warmth spreads through my entire body and I feel the dampness between my thighs, soaking my panties. Tonight isn't the night to let any thoughts cloud my mind. It's about one thing and one thing only—getting what I want. All inhibitions need to be let go.

Sliding my hands under the bottom hem of his shirt, I slowly begin to push it up his torso. His skin is warm under my palms as I continue to push his shirt up until I'm sliding it over his head. I toss it onto the floor with my clothes and begin to trail my fingertips over the planes of his body. His chest is solid and firm, just like I had imagined with him being an athlete.

I know that he works out, but as my fingers move across his abs, I smile to myself as I feel that he's not completely stacked. He has more of a lean, athletic build than anything. You wouldn't know it, though, with the way Hayden walks around like his shit doesn't stink.

That's just my bitterness talking, because even though he isn't ripped, he still has a body that was perfectly chiseled by God himself.

"Tell me what you want, pretty girl," Hayden

murmurs, bringing his lips back to mine. He traces the outline of my lips with the tip of his tongue before drawing my bottom lip between his teeth. As he lightly clamps down, I can't hold back the moan that slips from me.

Hayden releases my lip, running his tongue over the crescent shapes he left in my flesh. His hands find my waist, pulling me flush against him. We're half naked, chest to chest, my breasts pressed against him. It feels too hot in here... almost like we need to lose more clothing to cool down.

"I want you," I tell him, breathing against his lips.

"You got me," he murmurs, sliding the tips of his fingers under the waistband of my shorts. "I told you. I'm yours for the night, but only for the night."

"That's perfectly fine with me," I smirk, staring up into his eyes through the darkness. "Because I don't want any more than this one night with you."

"So, we're on the same page then," he nips at my bottom lip as he slides his fingers along my waist. He reaches for the button of my jean shorts and slowly slides it through the hole before pushing down the zipper.

I mimic his movements, reaching for the waistband of his shorts at the same time. He has basketball shorts on, so there aren't any buttons or zippers to mess with. Instead, I begin to push them down his thighs, along with his boxers. "I know how you operate, King," I breathe, pushing them as far as I can before they just fall down the rest of the way, pooling around his feet.

He hesitates for a moment, almost as if I caught him off guard and he's faltering. Wrapping my hand around the back of his neck, I bring his lips back to mine and this time I'm the one who's doing the claiming. Hayden moves his mouth with mine, our tongues tangling as he shoves down my shorts, pushing down my panties with them.

We're both completely naked, breaking apart as we kick off our shoes and collapse onto the air mattress together. Thankfully it holds under our weight and doesn't deflate with the way we land on it, practically on top of one another.

"You're sure this is what you want, baby?" Hayden questions me softly, his eyes searching mine.

I appreciate him asking for my consent, but if I didn't want it, we wouldn't be in this position. Narrowing my eyes at him, I stare up at him as he settles between my legs. "I said yes already. Now, stop wasting time by asking me stupid fucking questions, King."

He stares down at me for a moment, a smirk tugging on the corners of his lips as a sinister look passes through his eyes. I can barely see him in the darkness of the tent, but I can feel the need rolling off of him in waves.

And I need him just as badly.

————

HAYDEN

I don't bother asking her how she knows my name, because in this moment, none of that matters. My face dips down to hers, our mouths collide as she wraps her arms around the back of my neck. She tastes like the worst decision I've ever made and I know there will be hell to pay for it. Her lips part as I slide my tongue along the seam of them, slipping into her mouth as I devour her.

Settling between her legs, the tip of my cock presses against her pussy. She's already wet—fucking drenched—and I can't help myself as I moan into her mouth. Abruptly, I pull back for a moment, my eyes searching hers as I slowly push the head into her. Her fingers slide through my hair as she grips the back of my head, bringing my face down to hers. Our mouths crash into one another, her legs wrapping themselves around my waist as she pulls me closer.

Shifting my hips, I ease farther into her, feeling how tight she is around me as I fill her. A soft moan slips from her lips and I swallow the sound as I breathe her in. Our mouths melt together as I thrust into her, filling her to the brim.

I swear to God, I know her. I have no idea from where, but there's something so familiar about her. I know this girl has never been in my bed before and I can't quite put my finger on where I would know her from. Whether it's the sound of her voice or the way she carries herself...

I don't know how to explain it, but it's almost as if my soul knows her. She just makes complete sense to me. But then again, it could just be the alcohol in my system talking too. It may be cocky to say, but there's so many girls that are on my dick, it's hard for any of them to hold my attention for long.

But this girl—she has my undivided fucking attention right now.

Shifting my hips again, I slowly pull out, leaving just the tip in as I slam back into her. Our mouths break apart and she cries out in ecstasy, her nails digging into my scalp as I begin to piston my hips, driving my cock into her over and over again. Sliding my hands down to her ass, I lift her up, giving myself deeper access as I thrust into her once more.

She takes every thrust in stride, her hands falling to my shoulders as she begins to dig her nails into my flesh. I know there will be marks on my back in the morning and the thought alone has a smirk playing on my lips. I want her to leave her mark on me, just like I intend on doing to her. I don't know who the fuck this girl is, but I'm going to make sure she doesn't fucking forget me.

Because there's no way I'm going to be able to erase this night from my memory.

Abandoning my inhibitions, our surroundings fade and I let myself get lost in her. This mystery girl, the one that I won't see again after tonight. And since we only have one night, I'm going to make the most out of this moment I get with her.

I thrust into her again and she's writhing under my touch. My fingers dig into her ass as I grip her flesh, pounding into her over and over. She's so delicate, it feels like I could split her in two, but she takes it like she was built for me. I want this to last, but I know that I'm pushing both of us closer and closer to the edge. My balls are already constricting, drawing closer to my body when she abruptly stops me.

She drives her hands against my chest, planting her palms against me as she stares up at me. We're both breathless, lost in each other as we attempt to catch our breaths. Tilting my head to the side, my eyes bounce back and forth between hers, searching for whatever is wrong.

She gives nothing away, instead a look of frustration passes through her eyes. "Roll over," she demands, attempting to shift her weight to flip me over with her legs wrapped around my waist.

A smirk forms on my lips and I grip her ass harder, my cock still inside her as I roll onto my back. The air mattress shifts under our weight, groaning from the movement. I'm sure if there's anyone within earshot of this tent, they can definitely hear us in here right now. Shit, I wouldn't be surprised if they could hear us back at the party.

The roles are reversed and she's now on top of me, her pussy clenching around me as she stares down at me with a look of satisfaction. She got what she wanted and it's written all over her face, how pleased she is that she got her way. She may think she's in control, but it's all a facade. We might be in her tent and her bed, but I'm the one who is running shit here.

Gripping her hips, I attempt to top her from the bottom, but she fights against me, pinning me down with her hips every time I try. A chuckle vibrates in my chest and I let her have it, relaxing as she begins to ride me. She wants to be in control and the only reason that's happening now is because I'm letting it.

It doesn't last for long, though, because I can't fucking help myself. My hands are around her waist, my hips lifting to meet her with every thrust. We're both out of breath, climbing closer and closer to the edge as we move in tandem together. A warmth spreads across the pit of my stomach as I thrust into her once more.

My balls constrict and her pussy clenches around me, her orgasm tearing through her body as she comes apart on my cock. I'm right behind her, but quickly pull my dick out of her before I come. Wrapping my hand around the base, I pump my fist once before coming across her stomach. She inhales sharply, the warm, sticky fluid painting across her skin.

I'm mesmerized for a moment, completely transfixed by the sight of her now straddling my waist. Her soaked pussy is on my stomach and I swear to God, it feels like my dick could get hard again. I'm not quite sure she'd be ready for round two. I'm riding a wave of ecstasy as she climbs off me and rises to her feet, getting off the air mattress.

She bends down, reaching for something from the floor of the tent. I watch as she grabs my shirt and wipes my cum off her stomach before tossing it at me. I just barely catch it as I sit up on the mattress. I'm thrown off by her actions and I tilt my head to the side as I watch her continue to pick up clothing and toss them at me.

"You can see yourself out, right?" she questions me as she pulls her shirt back over her head and motions to the flap of her tent.

I'm speechless, completely at a loss for words as I pull my boxers and shorts back on. My shirt is covered in cum, so there's no way I'm putting that shit back on to walk back to the party. We agreed this was a one-time thing and I guess that our moment has come to an end.

But fuck me, if that wasn't one of the best moments I've had in a long time. Dare I say, quite possibly one of the best moments I've ever had with a girl.

She doesn't say another word as she climbs back

into the sleeping bag and pulls it up to her chin before laying her head down on the pillow. I glance down at her once more but words fail me as she lifts her head and cuts her eyes at me. She's acting cold and indifferent now, but I saw her in the moment. I fucking felt her while I was balls deep inside of her.

She's dangerous and I fucking love it. The fight for control and the challenge. She's literally everything I would look for in a girl, if I was in the habit of falling into relationships. Thank God, that's not my style. I'm more of a hit-it-and-quit-it guy and with the way she's looking at me right now, she threatens to destroy that entire code I live by.

I've never had a girl look at me like I wasn't handcrafted by God and for some reason, it's making me feel drawn to her like a moth to a goddamn flame.

I don't know who the fuck this girl is and I'm glad for that.

Because after this—I'm not so sure I want to see her again.

CHAPTER ONE
EDEN

THREE MONTHS LATER

My skates effortlessly glide across the ice and I'm lost in the music as I perform my freestyle routine. The other skaters are working on their own, none of us paying attention to one another as we move across the rink. An old-school hip-hop song plays through my AirPods. Even though they play music while everyone is skating, I prefer to listen to my own.

Plus, I'm not here to converse with anyone, so it doesn't matter that I can't hear a single word that is spoken to me. I think that after being here at Wyncote for three years, most of the other skaters know the deal with me. I'm here for one thing and one thing only—to skate.

Gearing up for the next move in my routine, I spin around, skating backward. Glancing behind me, I make sure that there is no one in my way. The Lutz is one of the hardest moves to execute perfectly, but it happens to be the one thing I've got down to a precise science. If I'm able to use my edge correctly on the entry into my jump, I should be able to nail it every single time.

Although, things don't always work out the way you plan it.

Moving into the takeoff position from the back outside edge of my skate, I use a toe pick and effort-lessly lift my skates from the ice as I soar through the air. My body spins and I land perfectly on my opposite foot. My edges are perfect as I land on the outside edge and throw my leg into the air, my body in a straight line.

My chest heaves with every breath that I take, my legs aching as I power through the pain and finish the rest of my routine that I have mapped out in my head. I don't miss some of the looks that the other girls give me as I skate past them, stopping as I reach the boards.

Glancing up at the scoreboard, I notice that our

time is up and the other skaters are already clearing off the ice as the Zamboni begins to make its way into the rink. I grab my skate protectors and carry them over to the door with me. Sliding them onto my skates, I step off the ice and make my way down the tunnel.

Since it's just a practice night for the hockey team, we're able to use the locker room that is reserved for the away team. It's actually fairly annoying. The hockey program is what essentially keeps the school going here, but they have a great figure skating program, as well. It just seems like we're not as prioritized as the hockey team.

They have a whole-ass locker room—we can't even get a small little area of our own. Instead, we have to use the other locker room or take turns in the bathroom. Honestly, it's bullshit, but who am I to be the one to change anything? Even though I may be the best skater that this school has, my word doesn't mean shit.

The figure skating program doesn't bring in the revenue like the hockey team does and that's what it always comes down to—money. So, we're left with no choice but to bow down to the team like they're gods, like the rest of the school does.

There's only one problem with that...

I refuse to get on my knees for any man.

Slipping into the locker room, I take off my skates and carefully put them back in my bag before sliding my feet into my white Chucks. Pulling out my phone, I turn off my music and take my AirPods out before putting them back in their case. As I shrug on my coat, Winter walks over to me with a grin creeping onto her lips.

"Okay, I know you have a strict policy of not talking to anyone while you're on the ice... but your skates are off so can we talk now?" She pulls the hair tie from her long, sable-colored hair before flashing her white teeth at me.

I've become friends with a few of the people I skate with, but that's about it. I have no time for anyone who doesn't have a common interest with me. It's just one of the things I've settled into in life. Why waste my time and energy on someone who isn't going to serve a positive influence in my life?

Winter, on the other hand... I met her freshman year. We ended up being roommates, which was perfect because we're both figure skaters. I tried to resist her at first, but she was persistent and inserted herself in my life. And she's been stuck to my side since then. She's the person I know I can rely on. My best friend.

"Yes, Winter," I laugh, shaking my head at her as I roll my eyes. "We're off the ice, so I'm listening now."

"I just wanted to say, you fucking killed it today. I can't wait to see you do your thing this weekend," she adjusts the strap of her bag over her shoulder as I grab my bag and step toward her. "Seriously, that Lutz was flawless. I still can't get my edges right when I takeoff."

Most of the other skaters have already left the room, so we are the last two to exit. I glance over at Winter as she pauses by the door. "You gotta shift your weight onto the back outside edge. I've seen how you do it and you're not putting enough weight on it to achieve the spin that you're going for. Tell you what, I'll listen to their garbage music on Wednesday and work with you on it."

Winter gasps, her expression completely exaggerated as she throws her hand over her chest and shoulders the door open. "Oh my god. Did Eden Finley just say that she's going to actually pay attention to something other than herself while skating?"

Rolling my eyes, I give her the middle finger as I step past her into the hallway. My gaze is still over my shoulder as I look back at her and I don't see where I'm going until I run into something solid. It's a warm, firm body that smells like disgusting hockey gear. I'm thrown off-balance and stumble backward as I attempt to catch my footing. My skate bag is awkward and doesn't help the situation.

A pair of hands reach out, grabbing my biceps as he helps to steady me on my feet. "I'm so sorry," he says breathlessly, his voice sounding like velvet as it touches my eardrums. "I wasn't paying attention and didn't see you there."

The air leaves my lungs in a rush as the sound of his voice registers in my mind. It's still hazy, a little fuzzy from the night that I heard it, but the warmth that spreads through my body reminds me of exactly who he is. Lifting my gaze to his, I meet his deep green eyes and Hayden King stares back at me, his eyes widening as he really sees me.

"It's you..." he practically whispers, his voice rough as his eyes bounce back and forth between mine in confusion. "I've been looking for you since that night."

I swallow roughly, lifting my chin as I stare up at him. I knew who Hayden was that night, but he had no idea who I was and I wanted to keep it that way. There's always been a sense of animosity between the figure skaters and the hockey players here. If he knew who I really was, there was no way that night would have happened. And even though it was a mistake, I was in the mood for a bad decision and Hayden King fit the bill.

"You must not have been looking that hard, because I've been right under your nose the entire time."

Hayden tilts his head to the side, staring at me through the cage of his helmet. Stepping backward, I shake my arms out of his grip, watching as his hands fall down to his sides. He crosses them over his chest defensively as he narrows his eyes on me.

"So, this is why you didn't want me to know your name, huh?" he muses, a smirk tugging on the corners of his lips. "It didn't make sense to me then, but now it does. You're a figure skater."

"Eden," Winter's voice sounds from behind me and I can hear the curiosity in her tone.

Hayden's face softens, his bright green eyes staring directly through mine. "Eden Finley. I know exactly who you are." His throat bobs as he swallows hard. "I've heard your name before, but never knew your face. Rumor has it, you're the best figure skater we have here."

"It's not just a rumor," I clip, the venom dripping

from my tongue as I cross my arms over my chest to match him. "That's exactly what I am. And exactly why that night was a goddamn mistake."

"Why?" he questions me, straightening his head as he squares his shoulders. "Because you figure skate and I play hockey?"

"Glad we're on the same page," I quip, my eyes narrowed as I glare at him. "Bye, Hayden."

Spinning on my heel, I turn to face Winter who stares at me like she has no idea what the hell just happened. My nostrils flare, my chest rising as I inhale deeply and attempt to shake off the memory of Hayden's hands on my skin that night.

"Eden, wait," he calls out after me as I walk past Winter, heading in the opposite direction of the rink. Hayden jogs after me, fully suited in his gear and skates. His hand darts out, grabbing my wrist to stop me.

"Let me go, Hayden," I demand, turning around to face him as I rip my arm away from him. "It was a one-night thing that we can just go back to pretending never happened. Okay? Okay, perfect."

Hayden stares at me for a moment, his eyebrows drawn together as his lip curls upward in distaste. Rolling his eyes, he shakes his head at me. "Typical.

You know, you really do fit the stuck-up cliché figure skater mold."

"And you're no different. The fuckboy, hockey player whose ego is bigger than his dick."

One of the guys behind Hayden snorts and Winter is by my side, ushering me away from him. I don't miss the look in Hayden's eyes, like I hit him exactly where it hurt. A wave of pain passes through his irises before they turn to ice.

With my back turned to him, I don't bother chancing a glance in his direction again as Winter leads me away and back into the main hallway. As soon as we're out of sight of them, she stops and turns to face me, her expression demanding an explanation.

"What the hell was that?"

I shrug. "A drunken mistake from the summer."

Winter tilts her head to the side. "You hooked up with Hayden over the summer? How did I not know this? And please tell me you knew who he was."

"I did," I admit with indifference. "I was in the mood to make a bad decision and he was there. He had no idea who I was then, but now he does. I wasn't exactly proud of it, so I didn't tell you. But it happened and it's not happening again."

"Good lord," Winter breathes, shaking her head

in disbelief. "You know how those hockey guys are. Total players. Good for you, girl. He's the last thing that you need to get wrapped up in."

A soft chuckle falls from my lips and I offer her a smile. "Trust me, that is something that is never happening."

"I didn't mean to drag you away like that, but, girl, I saw the fire in your eyes and I know what's coming after that." Winter links her arm through mine as we begin to walk down the hallway, toward the exit. "Damage control before you exploded."

"I appreciate it, because you know how I feel about those guys. The entire school acts like they walk on fucking water. When in reality, they only skate on ice, just like the rest of us. They're not the gods like everyone paints them to be and it's time that they're put in their place."

Winter laughs lightly. "I'm pretty sure you knocked him down a peg or two."

"Let's just hope he stays there."

As we exit the building and make our way out to our cars, I can't shake the memory of Hayden from that night. He's not someone I would ever get involved with—not with his reputation—and he's essentially my sworn enemy. But that doesn't erase the way he made me feel that night. Like for once he wasn't a god, but a mortal.

He worshiped me that night like I was his goddess.

And it can never happen again.

CHAPTER TWO
HAYDEN

What the hell was that?

I stand in the hallway near the tunnel, still staring off to where I saw Eden disappear with her friend. How the hell could I have been so stupid? She said my name that night and I didn't bother to question her on how she knew it. Of course, she knew me. It all makes complete sense now and I feel like a complete idiot.

There's always been a weird disconnect between the hockey players and figure skaters. It's hard to explain and I don't know where it even originated from. It's not like we're competing against each other in any sense at all, but yet it's like we're enemies just by association.

I'll admit, the figure skaters here definitely get

the shorter end of the stick. Our school takes a lot of pride in the hockey team, so the figure skaters don't get much recognition. And they don't even have their own locker room or anything like that. They have to share what is already ours, which none of us are particularly happy about.

I don't know if it boils down to jealousy or what it is exactly, but the girls that figure skate have always come off as if they think they're better than us. And the same goes for the hockey players. I mean, if we're being real here, the school does treat us like royalty, so it's hard to not have that complex. I wouldn't say the hockey players look down on the figure skaters... but those girls give off the vibe that their noses are so high in the fucking air, that we're beneath them.

Either way... I definitely fucked with the enemy and I should not have done that.

It's not like she has anything on me or can do anything to retaliate. She was the one who propositioned me, and fuck me if that wasn't one of the best nights of my life. And I would most definitely be lying if I were to say I wouldn't do it again. Because if she wanted me in her bed again, I wouldn't hesitate.

Figure skater or not—there was something about Eden Finley that I can't seem to shake.

"Dude," Simon skates over to me as soon as I'm on the ice. "What did I miss? I heard Logan and August talking about you and one of the figure skaters getting into it."

An exasperated sigh leaves my lips as I slide my hands into my gloves and lazily hold on to my stick as I skate a circle around him. "You remember that party that Derrick had at the lake?"

Simon nods. "Wait, you slept with some chick and couldn't figure out who it was that night." He pauses, his eyes widening. "Tell me it wasn't Eden fucking Finley."

Sucking my lips between my teeth, I nod back at him. "Yep," I admit. "I had no idea who she was. I mean, I heard her name, but I didn't recognize her face."

"Damn, bro," Simon shakes his head, a chuckle vibrating from his chest. "I know you came in the middle of the season last year, but I thought you would have known better than to fuck with the figure skaters—especially her. Eden doesn't like anyone, except for Winter and, like, one other chick. Other than that, she's not known for being the nicest person. Especially to the hockey team."

"What's her deal? I know there's always that underlying animosity, but has someone done something to her personally?"

Simon shrugs. "I don't know. I know she dated Chance Orion her freshman year. They were pretty serious, but he was a senior and was drafted into the NHL after that." He pauses for a second, waving Logan over. "I think things ended between them after that."

"What's up?" Logan asks the two of us, glancing back and forth between us as he skates over.

"Orion and Eden Finley. She was cool before they broke up, right?"

Logan nods. "Yeah. I mean, she always had that weird chip on her shoulder, being a figure skater, but she was cool with everyone when they were together. After he dropped her like it was nothing, she wrote us all off, like we all broke her heart."

I stare back and forth between the two of them as they talk about the breakup from an outsider's perspective. So, not only is there the underlying animosity, but Eden Finley is a scorned woman. And one who was fucked over by a hockey player, no less.

"Orion talked a big game to her about their future, but we all knew he was blowing smoke up her ass. The minute he got his offer and accepted it, she was discarded and he moved on without looking back."

"That explains a lot," I murmur, thinking aloud as I grab a puck with my stick and slide it across the ice.

"Word of advice?" Logan offers as he steals the puck from me. "Keep your distance from Eden. Your little dispute in the hallway was nothing. You're better off not getting involved with her."

"I mean, it's not like I was trying to make her my wife or anything. We just had a good time, one that I wouldn't mind repeating."

Logan shakes his head before he skates off, leaving Simon and I standing there for a moment. "I'm not telling you what to do, but Logan's right. Eden only cares about herself and isn't going to let anyone slow her down again."

A smirk forms on my lips. "Well, it's a good thing that I'm just as selfish."

Simon rolls his eyes. "It's your funeral, bro."

I watch him as he skates off after the other guys, and I'm left behind with my thoughts. Personally, I've never done anything to Eden Finley, but if she wants to treat me like I'm the enemy, then two can play this game. The last thing I'm going to do is let a girl like her derail my plans and cloud my mind.

After the shit I pulled at my last school with the coach's daughter, I don't have time for the drama or the bullshit. And if Eden wants to give me the cold shoulder, then I need to take that as a sign and move on.

If only that were how I really felt...

She intrigues me and she's awoken something inside me that I've never felt before. She wants to play this little game and push me away, then she better believe that I'm going to push back. I'm going to break down every goddamn wall she has built up and shatter the ice around her.

Eden Finley has no idea what is coming for her.

And it's the one person she views as her personal enemy.

Me.

CHAPTER THREE
EDEN

After my run-in with Hayden, I've been trying to push him from my mind. Thankfully, I don't have any classes with him this semester, so it's not hard to avoid him. The only problem is at the ice rink. I just need to make sure that I don't chance seeing him again, because I know it isn't going to end well.

I may have been meaner to him than I should have been, but it's better that way. And what I said wasn't exactly a lie. I've heard the rumors of how Hayden ended up here in the middle of the season last year. He's your typical playboy. The ones who will play games with your heart and light you on fire just to watch you burn.

He's no different than Chance. And I swore that after that entire relationship blew up in my face that I would never get involved with a hockey player again. They're self-centered and selfish assholes. Each of them is here for the same exact thing. To play the best that they can with the hopes of going pro after graduation.

I knew that was Chance's main goal when I got involved with him, but I fell hard and fast for him. I was blind to what was right in front of my face. He made his empty promises to me and I believed every single one of them. He was a senior, while I was a freshman. He made it clear that he was shooting for the NHL after he graduated.

But he made those goddamn promises. The ones of how he would support my goals and dreams. How we would stay together, even after he ended up being drafted to a team. He promised me that we would find a way to make it work. All of the talks of our future, of getting engaged and married one day.

And then he threw it all away. As soon as he was drafted, he ended things with me like it was just some minor inconvenience. Like our relationship wasn't what he made me believe it was. I felt stupid, betrayed, and downright heartbroken when he did that to me.

Chance showed his true colors and he opened my eyes to how these guys truly operate. Not only do they think they're better than the figure skaters, but they don't see anything past the game they're playing. And everything else in their lives is just a different game they play. Chance played the fuck out of me and I would never let that happen again.

We had our fun and it can't happen again.

———

Winter is already waiting for me at the rink when I get there. The hockey team doesn't have practice tonight, thankfully, so we have the ice for a few hours to get our practice in. It wasn't anything scheduled, but our coach had it cleared that it was an open skate. Usually, the hockey guys don't show up to these things because none of the nets are out, so there's really no purpose here for them.

Plus, our time to work on our skating is just as important as theirs.

"You ready to teach me how to nail that Lutz?" Winter questions me as we both lace our skates. She's her typical peppy self and I'm still in a sour mood from my run-in with Hayden a few days ago.

"Yep." I smile up at her, pushing away the irritation that crawls under my skin. "I'm even going to leave my AirPods in my bag, so no temptation to ignore anyone else who's skating."

Winter laughs lightly, rising to her feet as she pulls her gloves over her hands. "I don't care if you ignore anyone else. I'm the only one who gets your attention today."

Rising to my feet, I follow her out to the hallway, where it's already empty. As we walk down the tunnel and to the ice, I see some of the other girls are already skating, working on their different routines. Winter and I both pause at the doorway, pulling off our skate protectors before stepping out onto the ice. I take Winter's protectors from her and skate over to the boards, where I hang them on the side for when we're done.

Soft classical music plays through the speakers and I smile over at Millie. She's one of the other girls I actually get along with and this kind of music is her style. She skates over to me, her skates cutting the ice as she abruptly stops in front of me.

"I hope you don't mind the music. I know it's not what you prefer, but it seemed like the best pick for everyone here." She shrugs, a shy smile on her face.

That's the thing I like about Millie. She's always thoughtful toward others, always giving them the benefit of the doubt. I don't think there's a mean bone in that girl's body.

"You don't have to worry about me, Mill," I smile at her, skating alongside her. "I'm good with whatever you want to listen to. And if this is what you like, then it's perfect."

She offers me a genuine smile before she takes off, stretching out her legs as she moves past two of the other skaters talking to one another. Millie is two years younger, so she's still one of the newer members on our team. She's not stuck-up like some of the others. And unlike Hayden's assumption of me, I don't fit in with those girls either.

I notice Winter on the other side of the ice, working through her warm-up routine as I continue to skate around. I'm not really here for myself today, although this is really my happy place. The one place in the world that silences my mind and allows me to be free. My skates glide effortlessly across the ice as I break out into my own freestyle routine, working through some of my moves as I wait for Winter.

The sound of the classical music situates itself

inside my soul and I close my eyes, letting my body move along to the rhythm as I glide backward. As I open my eyes, I see Winter watching me, waiting for my direction. Pushing off with one leg, I gain some momentum as I bring the other up in front of my body. My legs are in a split, my thigh pressed against my chest as I grab my ankle and the toe of my skate, breaking out into an I-spin.

My body spins for a few moments, time suspended in air as my hair whooshes around me. The cold air prickles my skin and a smile forms on my face as my surroundings spin. Releasing my leg, I drop it down, slowly decreasing my speed before coming to a halt.

I skate across the ice, over to Winter who is stretching her legs once again. "You ready to work on that Lutz?" I ask her, a smile forming on my lips as the peace from skating settles in my soul.

Winter nods eagerly and she's all ears as I begin to explain the mechanics of the move to her. I break it down in slow motion, as best I can, explaining how I use the edges of my skates for takeoff and the landing. We run through the move a few times. She watches, studying each time I do it, before attempting it herself.

She gets better with each try and manages to

stay on her skates the entire time, which is a feat in itself. You wouldn't believe the amount of strength and precision it takes to land a jump like this one. And we find ourselves landing flat on our asses more times than any of us would like to admit.

Skating in a large circle, I spin around and begin the fluid movement backward as I prepare for take-off. As I move past Winter, I make sure she sees the way I use the edge of my skate before propelling myself into the air. As I spin, I'm lost in the euphoric rush before hitting the ice with my opposite skate, landing it perfectly as I throw my leg behind me, straightening my spine.

Someone whistles from across the rink, the sound loud enough to hear over the music, and I spin around, skating toward Winter as I see her face scrunch up in distaste. Sliding to a stop in front of her, my eyes search hers and I raise an eyebrow. I know the Lutz I just showed her was perfect, so I'm a little confused by the look on her face.

"What the hell are they doing here?" Winter scoffs, directing her gaze across the ice as she nods her head.

Spinning around on my skates, I follow after her line of sight and see Hayden on the opposite end of the rink. He's standing there with Simon and Sterling, two other hockey players. They're not dressed in their gear, but instead wearing hoodies and sweats with just their skates and gloves on. Each of them has a stick in hand and a puck lies on the ice beside them.

Hayden grabs the brim of his baseball cap and flips it around on his head as he begins to skate away from the guys. I watch as he stickhandles the puck, effortlessly moving it across the ice with skill. My jaw tightens, my hands clenching into fists as I stare at them across the ice.

"Just ignore them," Winter offers as she skates in front of me to block my view. I can still see them across the ice, passing the puck back and forth as they laugh about something.

Hayden glances over in my direction, nodding his head as a smirk forms on his lips, and it sends me over the edge. This is supposed to be our time here, but leave it to them to come and ruin it.

These damn guys think they own the ice? Well, they're in for a rude awakening.

Winter shakes her head at me, attempting to discourage me from approaching them, but it's already too late. I skate past her, heading straight toward Hayden. He lifts an eyebrow, coming to a stop as he passes the puck to Simon, and turns to face me. Propping his stick up, he leans against it slightly as his lips tip upward.

Damn him for looking so good right now.

I can't think about that, though. Right now, he's invading my space and I need him gone.

CHAPTER FOUR
HAYDEN

Eden's golden eyes are pinned on me as she skates across the rink toward me. I hear Simon and Sterling snicker as I turn to face her head-on. Her eyes are narrowed, her jaw clenched, and a pink tint spreads across her cheeks. She looks cute when she's pissed off. I just can't wait to hear what kind of words are about to come out of that pretty mouth.

Her skates cut into the ice as she abruptly comes to a stop in front of me, putting her hands on her hips. I allow my eyes to travel the length of her body for a moment, noticing her toned legs through her black leggings. My gaze follows up her thin torso, over the curves of her body, before traveling across her face.

Her amber-colored hair is pulled back in a tight bun, revealing her perfectly symmetrical face. I can't fight the smirk on my lips as I notice her eyebrows drawn together, her plump lips pinched into a straight line as she glares at me.

"Hey, Eden," I offer, my tone playful as I smile back at her, the anger rolling off her in waves.

"You guys aren't supposed to be here right now."

Tilting my head to the side, I raise an eyebrow as I push away from my stick, gliding into her space. "It said open skate on the board. If I remember correctly, that means the ice is open for anyone to skate..."

Eden tilts her head back, her chest rising and falling with every angry breath she takes. "Your team has its reserved times for practice. You don't belong here right now."

"Sorry, pretty girl." I stare back at her, noticing the small golden flecks in her irises. "But the rink is big enough for both of us."

Eden scoffs, rolling her eyes because she's not as amused by this as I am. "Just stay out of my way."

"Hm," I muse, narrowing my eyes at her as she gives me a challenging look. "I'll try my best, but I can't make any promises."

I watch her chest rise and fall, her breathing

shallow. The scent of vanilla touches my nose and I resist the urge to reach out to her. She might hate me, but I'm intrigued. And the more she gives me her anger and challenges me, the more I want to play with her. Eden lets out an exasperated sigh before spinning on her skates.

My eyes follow after her as I watch her skate away. She looks so natural, like being on the ice is exactly where she belongs. There's a gracefulness to the way she glides across the frozen surface and I find myself mesmerized, lost in the way her body moves.

"You're playing with fire, King," Sterling mutters as he skates over to me. I glance over at him as he purses his lips and shakes his head. "Everyone knows that girl is colder than the ice beneath our skates. She'll burn down anyone who gets in her way."

"Who said I was getting in her way?"

Sterling raises an eyebrow. "You know what I mean. You might not be a threat to her skating career, but she doesn't waste her time on meaning-less interactions. I've seen her go off on people before, but she's out for blood with you."

A chuckle vibrates in my chest as I shrug at him. "I wonder why."

"Because you don't know how to leave shit alone."

I look at him, feigning innocence. "What am I really doing? Running into her the other day was just a fluke thing. And I'm not here to bother her today. Just taking advantage of free ice time."

"You knew she was going to be here."

A smirk plays on my lips. "I mean, we all use the rink here. I knew it was a possibility."

"Let him go, Barrett," Simon says as he checks him lightly, throwing him off-balance. "King will get tired of the little game he's playing and find a new toy."

Simon chuckles as he skates away, taking the puck with the blade of his stick before Sterling follows after him. My gaze is trained on the back of his head for a moment. I don't know if he has feelings for Eden or what his deal really is, but there's something weird going on here. He's so concerned with what I'm doing with her and I can't figure out why.

Ignoring the little voice inside of my head, the three of us find our space on the ice, away from the figure skaters as we pass the puck around. We work on our stickhandling and attempting to get the puck away from one another. None of us really need the practice and Sterling was one hundred percent right. I knew Eden would be here and I wanted an excuse to run into her again.

Simon and Sterling fight over the puck for a moment and I allow my eyes to wander to the other side of the rink. Eden is skating, acting like I don't exist, as she works on her various jumps. I don't know the names of them, but watching her in action has me completely blown away. Even though I can skate my ass off, there's no way that I could even attempt the things she's doing right now.

I'm completely captivated by the way she moves and I can't tear my eyes away from her.

"Yo, King," Simon calls out my name as he passes the puck to me. I look up, watching it as it slides toward me, but I don't catch it fast enough. It moves past me, hitting the boards behind me before moving toward the other side of the ice.

Shit.

The puck slides right past Eden, coming to a stop along the boards, directly behind where she and Winter are skating. I glance over at Simon, who's staring at me with a smirk. Sterling looks slightly annoyed, but I ignore his expression as I shrug at Simon.

"I'm not going into the lion's den," Simon shakes his head quickly, his eyes wide.

"Go ahead, Hayden," Sterling nods over to the puck, raising an eyebrow. "You wanted to come here, you go get the puck."

Unable to bite my tongue, I quickly move my feet, skating over to him until I stop in front of him. We stand almost eye to eye, although I'm a few inches taller. Tilting my head to the side, I narrow my eyes at Sterling. "You got something with Eden? If you do, say it now and I'll leave it alone."

Sterling's eyebrows tug together and he glares back at me. "Did I once say anything about her? I just saw the shit she went through with Orion. I don't want to see her get hurt again."

"You care about her," I state, not bothering to question him because I know it's the truth based on his response. "Why? Who is she to you?"

"No one now," he says quietly, a pained look passing through his brown eyes. "We used to be friends. Before she wrote us all off, like we were behind their breakup."

I glance over at Simon for confirmation and he nods. As I look back at Sterling, my eyes are still narrowed on his. "Just friends, though? Nothing more?"

"Some of us can be friends with girls without feeling the need to fuck them," Sterling snaps at me. "So, yes. We were just friends and never anything more than that. No need to worry about breaking the fucking bro code," he clips, as he turns his back on me and faces Simon.

"I'm out of here," he tells Simon before skating toward the door and stepping off the ice. My gaze follows after him before I look back at Simon.

"They were close," Simon shrugs. "But he's not lying. They were never more than friends, and he's just looking out for her in that way."

I raise an eyebrow at him. "Why would he do that if she hates you guys?"

"Because she's not the ice sculpture she appears to be."

My lips part as I attempt to form a response, but I'm interrupted as a delicate arm wraps around my chest. I look down at her small hand, pressing the puck against my chest. As I spin around, Eden keeps her hand there, holding the black puck over my sternum.

"I told you to stay out of my way." Her voice is low, her tone ice cold as she stares up at me with her bright, golden eyes.

Lifting my hand, I place it over hers, holding her

against me for a moment. Her throat bobs as she swallows hard, her eyes glossy before she snaps out of it. Jerking her hand away from my chest, I catch the puck as it begins to fall.

"I was nowhere near you."

She raises an eyebrow at me. "This is your puck, isn't it?"

Flipping the puck around in my hand, I pretend to inspect it before looking back up at her. "It might be. It's hard to tell, though. You know, they all look the same."

Eden snorts, rolling her eyes at me. "Keep it over there, because next time I won't be returning it."

"You can keep it now as a memento, if you'd like," I offer, a smirk playing on my lips as I hold it out for her. "Something to remind you of me."

"I'd rather forget you than remember a single thing about you, Hayden King."

A chuckle vibrates in my chest and Eden's eyes slice to mine. She acts like she doesn't want to remember, but I know by the look in her gaze that she remembers everything that happened between us that night. The way she moved underneath me as I drove her body into a state of ecstasy that it's never experienced before.

"Good luck with that, baby," I murmur, leaning

toward her ear as I skate past her. "Although, if you want a reminder, you know where to find me now."

"I'm not like the other girls you've fucked around with," Eden quips, spinning on her skates to face me as I stop behind her. "Your words don't have the same effect on me."

"My words might not, but you haven't seen what I can do with my tongue yet."

Eden rolls her eyes as she begins to skate backward. "In your dreams, King."

I watch her as she effortlessly spins around, her back facing me as she meets up with Winter. The two of them skate over to the boards, grabbing their skate protectors before making their way off the ice. Standing in place, I stare after her until she disappears from my line of sight.

She might think she's made of ice, but she's in for a rude awakening.

I plan to melt away every frigid layer that encapsulates her.

CHAPTER FIVE

EDEN

After Hayden and his hockey friends interrupted our open skate, I haven't seen him since. That was over a week ago. I've more so been avoiding any chance of running into him. Anytime I am at the rink, I make sure I am out of there before the hockey team shows up for practice. Either that or I hide out in the locker room until I know they're all already on the ice.

It's pathetic—I know. But that's the position Hayden has put me in. It sounds simple to say that I could just easily ignore him if I were to run into him again, but that's not the case. There's something about him that entices me and he knows how to get a reaction out of me.

Plus, that guy is goddamn relentless. He

wouldn't let me get away without getting a word in, even if I wanted to.

Winter is waiting for me in her car at the end of the day. We usually carpool to campus on the two days our class times match up and when we have practice. That's one of the added benefits of living with my best friend. She's an easygoing housemate and she prefers to drive.

"You want to go do something tonight?" she asks as I toss my bag into the back seat and pull my seat belt across my chest. "We could go get dinner and drinks or something?"

I weigh my options between her plans and the ones I already had floating around in my head. Go get dinner with her or sit at home and watch TV with a carton of ice cream.

"Yeah, that sounds like a plan to me. It is Friday, after all, and thankfully we don't have to be up for anything in the morning."

"You know, as soon as competitions start again, our weekends are going to be full," she reminds me as she pulls her car out of the parking lot and onto the street. "We might as well enjoy our free time while we can."

I glance over at her, offering her a smile. "Hey, at least it keeps us out of trouble, right?"

Winter snorts, rolling her eyes at me. "I happen to like a little bit of trouble every now and then." She pauses for a moment, raising an eyebrow at me. "And apparently, you do too."

"Nope, we're not talking about him," I interject, cutting her off before she can take the conversation any further. Winter has already tried to get all of the juicy details from our one-night stand. I told her the bare minimum, but enough that I thought it would keep her satisfied. I must have been wrong.

"Oh, come on, Eden." She sighs, pulling the car into the parking lot of our apartment building. "No one said you have to marry the guy. If you had fun with him that night, there's no harm in doing it again."

"In case you hadn't noticed, I kind of can't stand the guy... and he plays hockey, which is even more of a turn-off."

Winter parks the car and kills the engine before looking at me skeptically. "Right. God forbid that you get involved with someone who plays," she pauses, and gasps, "hockey."

Grabbing my bag from the back seat, I climb out of the car and slam the door shut before my eyes slice to hers. "This is Hayden King we're talking about. I know you've heard the rumors about him. Seriously, he's a player and a pig."

"Whatever you say," Winter throws her hands up in defeat as we walk into the building and to the door of our apartment. "All I'm saying is, this is our last year here. Enjoy it. And stop making enemies with everyone you dislike."

"Yes, Mom," I roll my eyes, pushing past her as she opens the door. "I'll be in my room, so let me know when you're ready to go."

Winter mumbles something under her breath, but I don't quite hear her as I walk down the hallway and into my bedroom. This is where the two of us differ. Winter is a people pleaser; she makes friends with everyone. I'm the opposite. I don't need to be friends with everyone that I meet. And if I make some enemies along the way, so be it.

It's not my fault Hayden ended up being one of those people.

———

After our little disagreement earlier, we both went to our separate rooms and when it was time to leave, it was as if it never happened. That's one of the things I like about our friendship. We can disagree and have our little arguments, but there's nothing that can come between Winter and me. She's more like a sister than anything, and that's just part of what comes with living with her.

All of the restaurants already had their tables full and we were both too hungry to get on any type of a wait list. So, instead, we ended up at one of the sports bars, which wasn't my idea. It was Winter's, but I decided to go along with it anyway.

They didn't have any open tables, so we ended up having to sit at the bar. I would have rather had a table, but I think Winter's main goal is to get drunk while we're here, so this works too. She's smart enough to know that she needs to put some food in her stomach, though, before she starts pounding drinks.

"What's up, girl?" I ask her as she drains more than half of her margarita in one sip. Winter likes to drink, but only at this rate when she's really stressed out about something.

Winter looks over at me, tucking her long black hair behind her ears as her hazel eyes find mine. An exasperated sigh slips from her lips as her shoulders sag slightly. "My parents are coming to visit next weekend and I'm really not looking forward to seeing them."

"Why not?" I've met her parents before and they've always seemed to be nice. Winter never spoke of anything bad happening between them, so I'm a little confused about why she suddenly doesn't want to see them.

"They're planning on getting a divorce and I'm pretty sure they're only coming to see me to tell me about it." She pauses for a moment, shrugging in an attempt to seem indifferent as she takes another sip of her drink. "I'm honestly not that bothered by it. It's been a long time coming, but I'm worried about my little sister. She's only a junior in high school, and now everything's going to change for her."

"Are they bringing Mia along with them?"

Mia has come to visit us a few times, but their parents were always weird about her staying for too long. They know we live in a college town, but it's not like we have ever tried to expose Mia to that side of the college life. Even though she had been persistent about it each time she was here.

"Yeah, I think so. I don't know if she knows or not, so I don't want to say anything to her about it until they decide to drop the bomb on us."

"I'm sorry, Winter," I tell her with nothing but sympathy. I don't know how she feels going through this and I can't even imagine. My parents are still happily married and I don't know what I would do if they decided to split up, even though I'm grown up and out of the house now.

"It's fine," she mutters, waving her hand dismissively before she drains the rest of her drink. "Let's just get drunk and forget about all of our troubles?"

A smile spreads across my face and I nod as I wave the bartender over. "Two more margaritas, please. And keep them coming."

The bartender nods, chuckling as he walks over to make our drinks. Winter falls silent for a moment, but as soon as our drinks are back in front of us, she perks up. Grabbing the glasses, we hold them together.

"To a night of forgetting!" Winter exclaims as we tap the rims together and both take a sip. It isn't long after that when she is complaining about how we should have done it with shots instead.

Shaking my head at her, I sip my margarita at a slower pace, but it isn't long before we're ordering another round and are well on our way to being drunk. We did agree that it was the night to forget all of our troubles, so what the hell? I'll drink until my memory is completely fuzzy.

Winter falls into an easy conversation with some guy sitting next to her. My eyes scan the room as I fall into the silence around me, even though the bar is pretty loud by this hour. I watch as everyone converses and laughs with the people they're with. And for the first time in a long time, I feel alone in a room full of people.

Lifting my glass to my lips, I take another sip of my margarita before setting it back down. The scent of cologne drifts into my nose and I close my eyes, inhaling deeply as it takes me back in time. His breath is warm against my ear, his chest just barely brushing against my back.

"What are you doing here, pretty girl?"

CHAPTER SIX
HAYDEN

Walking into the bar with Simon and Greyson, we find an open high-top table since the bar is already full by this time at night. Our practice ran a little late and this was the place all our teammates frequented after practices and games. And since it's a Friday night, it only seemed fitting to come here to have a few drinks.

What I didn't expect to see was Eden...

We order our drinks and I don't make a move in her direction—not yet, at least. She didn't see us when we walked in and I've never seen her here before, so I can imagine that we're the last people she's expecting to see. Instead, I sit back in my chair and drink a few beers with the guys, watching her from a distance.

Eden is sitting at the bar with Winter, but it isn't long before Winter is talking to the guy sitting next to her. Simon and Greyson are talking about some chick from their one class, but I have them tuned out and neither of them seem to notice. I can't seem to take my eyes away from Eden as I watch her in curiosity.

She's sitting at the bar, slowly sipping her margarita as she looks around at the different people surrounding her. It's almost like she's not really here, though—instead just lost in her own head and consumed by her own thoughts.

What I wouldn't give to see what's going on in that pretty little head of hers...

We order another pitcher of beer and I can feel the alcohol already working its way through my system. I'm not drunk, but I definitely have a nice buzz going, judging by the way my body feels warm and I feel an overwhelming sense of happiness. Although, I must admit, I'm bothered by the way Eden looks right now.

She still looks around at the other people, almost like she doesn't feel like this is where she belongs. And even though she puts up her wall of ice whenever someone attempts to get close, she looks fucking lonely. It's not something I've ever seen on her before. It almost looks as if the light in her eyes has dimmed, and I don't like it.

I want to see them shine, even if it's with irritation and it's directed at me.

"I'll be back," I tell the guys as I rise to my feet. Greyson simply nods, since he never likes to get involved in anyone's business. Simon raises an eyebrow, his gaze following mine as I nod to Eden at the bar. I don't miss the crooked grin on his lips as he shakes his head and directs his attention back to Greyson.

Leaving the two of them at the table, I make my way over to the bar. Eden doesn't notice me as I step up behind her. Leaning in close, my chest brushes against her back as I inhale her faint vanilla scent.

"What are you doing here, pretty girl?" I whisper, my voice only for her to hear. Her body stills for a moment, her hand still wrapped around the stem of her glass.

"Hayden," she murmurs as I move beside her and slide into the now empty seat next to her. Eden looks over at me, her honey-colored eyes meeting mine. "Are you stalking me now?"

A smirk tugs on the corners of my lips. "I could ask you the same thing."

Her eyebrows tug together, her eyes glazed over slightly from the alcohol in her system. "What does that even mean? How was I supposed to know you would be here?"

"Because we've been coming here for years. It's where all of the guys usually go after practice or home games."

"Well, sorry," she clips, her tone sharp as the venom drips from her fangs. "I didn't realize you owned the place, King."

Her comment throws me off. Winter still hasn't noticed me sitting here and is too immersed in flirting with the guy beside her to even have a care. Does Eden feel that out of place right now that she needs to lash out at me?

"Can I ask you something?" I throw out to her before taking a sip of my beer.

Eden stares back at me for a moment. "I guess."

"What did I personally do to you to make you hate me so much?"

Eden's eyes widen for a moment, like my question came completely out of left field. I'm not saying that she's my favorite person or even that I want to be friends with her. I have no problem admitting that she's fucking gorgeous. There's something about her that keeps my attention and that's more than I can say for any other girl.

She shrugs dismissively. "Nothing, I guess. I just know who you are, I know your type, and I want nothing to do with someone like you."

"Fair enough," I agree with her, simply because I know that isn't what she wants. She wants me to argue back with her, to defend myself, but what's the point? Maybe Simon and Sterling were right and I just need to leave the damn girl alone.

I don't think that's possible.

"You don't like me, I'm fine with that," I tell her as I reach out to brush a piece of hair away from her face. Her skin is warm beneath my fingertips as I sweep them across her cheek and behind her ear. They linger for a moment before I drag them down the side of her neck. "But why does your heart race every time I touch you? Your breathing grows ragged and shallow. The pink tint on your cheeks. Whether you want to admit it or not, I have an effect on you that you can't resist."

Eden narrows her eyes for a moment before swatting my hand away from her. A chuckle falls from my lips as she picks up her drink and takes a long sip. "Careful, King," she warns, her voice husky and betraying her words. "Your arrogance is showing."

"I can show you more than just my arrogance, baby," I murmur, leaning closer to her, watching her throat bob as she swallows hard. "All you have to do is just say the word."

Her nostrils flare as she inhales deeply and clears her throat. "I told you that was a one-time thing, Hayden. It was a mistake and it never should have happened."

"And what did you learn from your mistake?" I ask her, still in her space as her scent invades my senses. "Did you learn how much you love making them with me?"

Her lips part slightly, a ragged breath slipping from them as her eyes bounce back and forth between mine. I watch as her chest rises and falls with every shallow breath she takes, like the oxygen is slowly being drained from the room and she can't get enough of it.

"What do you want from me, Hayden?" she questions me, her voice thick with lust as a fire burns in her eyes.

Leaning back, I grab my beer and lift it to my lips, watching her as she watches me. "One more night with you, Eden. I had a taste of you, but I haven't had my fill."

Eden stares back at me, her eyes slightly widening as my words sink in. I watch her throat again as she swallows hard, before pulling her bottom lip between her teeth. I want so badly to pull it away from her with my own mouth instead.

"One more night?" she responds, her voice quiet and her eyes hooded.

I nod, my eyes never leaving hers. "Give me one more night to fuck you out of my system and then we can act like this never happened. You can go back to hating me and we can go our separate ways."

"No strings attached, Hayden. If I agree to this, it doesn't mean we're friends or anything like that."

"Trust me, I'm not looking for a relationship or even a friendship," I assure her, even though the words taste bitter on my tongue. There's a part of me that wants to melt away her frosty exterior, but if she'll give me one more night in exchange for nothing, then I will take what I can get.

"Good," she muses as the corners of her lips lift upwards. "Because tonight feels like the perfect night to make another mistake with you."

CHAPTER SEVEN
EDEN

This is the exact reason why I fight so hard to stay away from Hayden King. I don't know why it is that he has the effect he does on me, but every time he's around and he tears my guard down, it's hard for me to resist him. There's something about the softness in his eyes, the parts of him he keeps hidden from the world and shields with his playboy facade.

I'm not saying he isn't a playboy, because I know about Hayden and his history. But there's a softer side, hiding behind the arrogance he constantly emits. There are layers to him, yet no one takes the time to notice. It's probably because he's too in your face with his cockiness, but I see through his bullshit.

I can't let myself get involved any deeper with him, though. Something about him reminds me of Orion and I think that's what scares me the most. Perhaps it's his persistence. When I first met Orion, I was just a baby in my freshman year. I didn't want to get involved with anyone and he was so goddamn insistent.

He worked his way under my skin like a splinter, but he was never permanent. I thought otherwise and didn't realize how disposable I was in his life. I will never be that in someone else's life again and I can't let myself think that Hayden is any different— because he isn't.

Like he said... one more night to fuck me out of his system. Maybe then his persistence will subside and I can successfully avoid him. Another mistake, another bad decision, and then I will finally learn my lesson. After tonight, I know I can't fall into this habit with him, and the thought will only make hating him easier.

But with the way he's looking at me right now with those hooded eyes, it's hard to imagine hating any part of him.

"How much have you had to drink?" he questions me, his voice low as his eyes search mine.

Rolling my eyes, I snort. "This is only my second one, King. I'm barely even buzzed."

A smirk tugs on his lips and he nods. "You might not think much of me, Eden, but the last thing I would do is take advantage of a girl when she's drunk."

"Is it really taking advantage if I'm giving my consent?"

Hayden shrugs. "If you're drunk, are you really in the right mind to give consent?"

"I appreciate you trying to be a gentleman, Hayden, but that's not what I'm looking for tonight," I tell him honestly as I take a sip of my margarita. "I want to make a mistake with you and hopefully fucking learn from it this time."

He stares at me for a moment, his tongue darting out as he wets his lips. "I hope we both learn, because I need you out of my system and out of my goddamn head."

His words feel like they throw me off balance. Still holding on to my glass, I take another large gulp, attempting to wash away the lump that lodges in my throat. Hayden already made it clear that he needed to get me out of his system and the sexual tension that sizzles between us whenever we're near each other is palpable.

But it's the end of his sentence that throws me off. He wants me out of his head. What the hell could I possibly be doing in there? We had a one-night stand over the summer and sure, we've had a few run-ins since then... but what could possibly be going on in that mind of his that involves me?

"So, what do you say, pretty girl?" Hayden questions me, tilting his head to the side as he sets down his empty beer. "You ready to get out of here?"

I glance over my shoulder at Winter before looking back at Hayden. "I came here with Winter," I explain to him, pulling my bottom lip in between my teeth. She knows Hayden and I slept together before, but I don't want to deal with her questions if she knows that I'm leaving with him now.

"And?" Hayden retorts, cocking an eyebrow at me before he looks over my shoulder at her. "It looks like she's a little preoccupied. Did you guys come here together?"

Releasing my bottom lip, I nod. "Yeah, she drove."

A smirk forms on Hayden's lips as he leans back in his seat and crosses his arms over his chest. "You don't want her to know you're leaving with me, do you?" A sinister look passes through his eyes. "You want me to be your dirty little secret, baby?"

My jaw clenches and I feel the heat creeping up my neck before spreading across my cheeks. I don't answer him, because that's exactly what I want him to be. At least just for tonight.

"Your place or mine?" I ask him.

A chuckle rumbles in his chest. "Babe, I live in a house with two other guys. There's no way we keep this a secret if I take you there."

"Yeah, well, I live with Winter, so how exactly is that going to work?"

"It's not ideal, but I'm not against fucking you in the back seat of my car."

Narrowing my eyes at him, my top lip curls up in distaste. "Gee, how thoughtful of you."

"What do you want? A bed covered in rose petals or some shit?" he quips playfully as he uncrosses his arms. I watch him as he rises to his feet and takes a step toward me, directly into my space. He leans down, his lips brushing against my ear. "I'll be out front waiting for you. You figure out how the hell you're getting away from your friend."

The warmth of his breath sends a shiver down my spine and he lightly presses his lips against the sensitive skin behind my ear. He trails his lips along my skin before nipping at my lobe.

"For the record, I'm not fucking you in my car,"

he breathes, his voice thick with lust. "I'm taking you back to your place and I'll sneak out when your roommate is asleep."

A fire ignites inside me, warmth spreading across the pit of my stomach. Instinctively, I clench my thighs together, inhaling as his scent invades my senses. He makes my head swim and I can't think straight with him this close. It could be from the alcohol, but it's more so him.

Hayden King is fucking intoxicating.

He pulls away, a ghost of a smile on his lips as he stares down at me, waiting for me to respond. "You gonna take care of your friend and meet me outside?" he asks as he lightly cups the side of my face, his thumb gently stroking my cheek.

Swallowing roughly, I nod as any words I had to say get caught in my throat.

Hayden smiles down at me, dragging his thumb across my skin once more. "Good girl." He winks, before pulling his hand away. Without another word, he spins on his heel and strides away from the bar, leaving me completely breathless.

My head is still swimming, my body tingling, and I feel like I could explode. Goddamn him. This is what Hayden does to me and I hate him for it. It makes me dislike him even more than I already do, just for the pure fact that my body betrays me anytime he's this close to me.

Lifting my glass to my lips, I drain the rest of my margarita before setting it down. A ragged breath escapes me and I inhale deeply, attempting to calm my heart as it thumps erratically in my chest. Turning around in my seat, I find Winter is still fully immersed in her conversation with the same guy.

My hand shakes, my palm clammy as I reach for her and tap on her shoulder. Winter turns around, the smile leaving her face as her gaze meets mine. The heat is still spread across my cheeks and her eyes scan my face.

"Are you okay?" she questions me, a worried look passing through her eyes. "You look flushed."

I nod, forcing a smile on my face. "I think I'm going to get an Uber and head home. I drank my drinks way too fast and feel pretty exhausted."

Internally, I cringe at the lie and the way it easily fell from my lips without any remorse. I hate leaving her here like this, but I recognize the guy she's talking to. I didn't notice at first, but it's someone she's been hanging out with occasionally. I can't remember his name for the life of me, though.

"Are you good to drive home?" I ask her, glancing over her shoulder at the guy beside her before looking at her. "Are you good here with him, too?"

Laughter falls from her lips. "Girl, I told you about Travis already." She pauses, tilting her head to the side. "Remember? He plays for the football team. We've hung out a few times and he's safe."

"If you're sure," I tell her, still feeling wary of leaving her. I do remember her telling me about him now, but you still never know. Then again, they are in a public place.

"Are you sure you don't want me to take you home? I can meet up with him another time," she tells me, sitting up straighter in her seat like she's about to shift into mom mode.

I shake my head at her, waving my hand dismissively. "Don't ruin your night over me. I already called an Uber, so I'm good."

"Okay. Well, I'll see you later tonight," she pauses, a grin tugging on the corners of her lips as she winks, "or in the morning..."

A soft chuckle escapes me and I can't help but feel a little more at ease. I can only hope that she'll be late getting home or coming home in the morning. That way I can get Hayden out of our apartment before she has the chance of catching him.

After saying my goodbyes to her, I go to pay my

tab, only to find out that Hayden already paid for it. My heart pounds erratically in my chest as I grab my purse and head out of the bar. Just as he promised, Hayden's black WRX is parked out front and the engine rumbles as he sits there waiting for me.

I can't see through the tinted windows, but he must be leaning over the center console because the door is suddenly pushed open for me. Grabbing the side of the door, I pull it open more before dropping down into the seat next to him.

A soft blue hue glows in the car from the lights inside as I close the door behind me. Grabbing my seat belt, I put it on before turning to look at him. Hayden has one hand on the steering wheel, the other on the gearshift, and his head is turned toward me.

"I was beginning to think you weren't going to come out."

"Was that a crack in your ego? The possibility that a girl was standing you up instead of melting into a puddle at your feet?" I quip, feeling the electricity in the air between us.

"Oh, no, baby." He smirks, shaking his head. "If you weren't coming out, I was coming back in for you."

My heart is in my throat and I attempt to push

away the stupid feelings he ignites inside me. He's a smooth talker, that's all Hayden King is. His words hold no weight.

"You better start driving before I change my mind."

A chuckle rumbles from his chest. Without another word, he moves the gearshift and the tires peel as he whips the car onto the street. The speed pushes my back against the seat and a rush of adrenaline courses through my body.

Hayden is dangerous and intoxicating.

This is most definitely a mistake.

And I can't wait to regret it in the morning.

CHAPTER EIGHT
HAYDEN

Eden gives me her address and I don't need the GPS to tell me where to go. The apartment building she lives in isn't far from campus and I've been there before. Thankfully, never to her apartment, but I ended up there one night with Simon. We were supposed to go hang out with some people, but the night ended with me going home and him falling into bed with some chick.

To be honest, the entire night was pretty lame and a blur after I started downing shots because I was that damn bored. Everyone knows me as the playboy, the fuckboy of the team, but little do they know that I don't fuck around like I used to.

After that night over the summer with Eden, I've only slept with two other chicks since then. Both were one-night stands and a way to distract myself from the chick that burrowed herself under my skin. I tried fucking her out of my system by burying myself in between someone else's legs, and it didn't work.

So this is my last option. The last resort. The only way to fuck her out of my system is to bury myself between her legs and hope that I come out alive.

There's something about Eden that draws me in. She's an enigma and I can't help but keep flying closer to the flame that burns inside her. I know I shouldn't because I'm bound to burn if I fly too close. But at this point, I would gladly go up in flames if it meant I could get her out of my damn head.

I'd never admit any of this aloud. Doing that makes it real and this can't be. None of these feelings can have the attention my mind has been giving them. Eden hates me and I'm only finding myself growing fonder of her. And I need that to stop immediately. I don't do feelings; I don't do relationships. It's a wham, bam, thank you, ma'am and I keep moving.

Yet, here I am coming back for fucking seconds like a starved man.

As I speed down the streets, I catch Eden grinning from the corner of my eye. She glances over at me, a wild look in her eyes as I shift lanes through the city. I'm breaking every traffic law, but I don't even care with the look on her face. She's as cold as the ice we skate on, but in this moment, she's more carefree than I've ever seen her.

Eden puts her window down as I shift into a higher gear, the car picking up speed. Her hair whips around in the wind, the air cold as it rushes in through the window. The lilt of her laughter is like music to my soul, snaking itself around my eardrums. She leans her back against the car door, tipping her head back to hang out the window as I continue to race toward her apartment.

She lifts her ass, like she's going to lift herself out the window with her seat belt still strapped around her. A rush of adrenaline hits me and I lift my foot from the gas slightly. My arm reaches out for her, my hand finding her thigh as I lean over the center console.

Her skin is warm through her leggings under my palm. Her thighs are toned from the endless hours of skating and I feel my cock growing in my pants as I run my hand along her leg, reaching for her hip. Eden lifts her head, looking down at me as she slides the top half of her body back into the car.

"What's wrong, playboy?" She smirks with a sinister gleam in her eyes. "I thought you were all about the wild side of life?"

My breath catches in my throat at the sight of her. Her cheeks are pink from the cold air, her wind-blown hair a tangled mess around her face. And I swear to God, I've never seen anything more fucking beautiful.

"As much as I like to test the limits of life, I don't want you falling out of my car."

My hand is back on her hip and I have no intention of letting her go. Eden settles back in her seat and I turn my attention to the road again. I begin to stroke her flesh through the material of her pants as I let the car fall to the speed limit. We're not far from her apartment now, but at this moment, I'd have no problem pulling over and fucking her on the side of the road.

Pushing my hand along her thigh, I push my fingers between her legs and she slowly parts them. I glance over at her from the corner of my eye and her eyes are trained on the side of my face, burning holes through my flesh. Inching my fingertips closer, I move along her leg until I feel the warmth of her pussy through her pants.

I slide my fingers along her, stroking her sensitive flesh through the material that's creating a barrier. A soft moan falls from Eden's lips and I glance over at her, watching as she draws her bottom lip between her teeth. My cock throbs and I see her apartment building about half a block away.

Stepping on the gas, I race toward the parking lot. Pulling my hand away from her, I shift gears, downshifting as I reach the entrance to the lot, and whip my car in. I pull into the first parking spot I find and throw it in park before killing the engine. Eden is already climbing out of her seat, pushing her door shut behind her. I'm right behind her, getting out of my side and locking the doors as I stride after her.

Eden unlocks the door to the building and we slip inside, heading straight toward the elevator. The lobby is empty and I'm not surprised at this time. It's already midnight, so whoever lives here is either in their apartments or they're not here. The elevator doors slide open and we step inside as Eden presses the button for the eighth floor.

As the doors close, I step behind her, grabbing her hips with my hands. Eden gasps as I spin her around to face me. Stepping with one leg between hers, I push her back to the wall of the elevator. Releasing her hips, I slide my hands up her body until I'm cupping the sides of her face.

"I don't know what it is about you, but you drive me fucking crazy."

Eden tilts her head to the side. "I like it better when you don't talk," she breathes, tipping her chin up to get a better look at me. "Your words mean nothing because I know I'm not the only one you've said them to."

I stare back at this crazy girl, half in disbelief. I know why she's under the impression that I would have said the same thing to other girls I've been with, but I haven't. Because none of them have ignited this fire inside me like she has.

"That's where you're wrong, baby," I murmur, dipping my face down to hers. "No one else but you."

Eden's eyes widen, her lips parting like she wants to respond, but I don't give her the chance. My mouth crashes into her, claiming her lips with mine as I steal the air from her lungs. Her hands find my sides, clutching onto my hoodie as I slide my tongue along the seam of her lips. She instantly opens, letting me in as my tongue slides along hers.

She doesn't fight against me to get the last word in. Instead, she lets me consume her. Our tongues tangle together as our mouths melt into one another's. I've never tasted anything sweeter than her. Everything about this girl scares the fuck out of me, but I've never been one to run away from danger.

The elevator doors slide open and I break away from her, taking a step back as I grab for her hand. She follows me out into the hall and I pause as I wait for her direction. Eden takes control, leading me toward her apartment. As we reach the door, she drops my hand, reaching into her purse for her keys. I step behind her, my hands finding her hips again as I drop my face down to her neck.

The smell of her light vanilla perfume invades my senses and I breathe it in, my eyes falling shut as I trail my lips along her neck. Eden sighs, her ass pressing against me as she fumbles with her keys. Nipping and sucking on her skin, I taste every inch that is exposed to me as she finally unlocks the door.

My hands are still on her hips and I follow her in as she pushes open the door. Using my foot, I kick it shut behind us, but Eden reaches around me, making sure to lock it. We're still in the small foyer area as I spin her back around to face me. I can't get enough of this girl. My hands slide through her hair as I grip the back of her skull and my lips find hers again.

Eden slides her hands under my shirt, pushing it up with my sweatshirt. Her hands are soft, sliding like silk over my skin as she runs them around my back. Guiding her with my hips, I hold her face to mine, our lips molded together as I back her through the apartment. I've never been in here before and have no idea where we're going, but it doesn't even fucking matter.

We make it into the kitchen and I'm backing her against the counter, our tongues tangled together as she runs her hands over my skin. She pushes my shirt and sweatshirt up farther. We break apart for only a moment as I pull them over my head and toss them onto the floor. I push her coat off her shoulders before reaching for the bottom hem of her shirt.

Eden doesn't resist as I lift her shirt over her head and drop it onto the floor. Her eyes search mine, a fire burning deep inside her irises as I strip her bra away from her body. This is the first time I'm seeing her in real light, since our first time was in the dark tent by the lake. She's fucking breathtaking and I literally cannot keep my eyes off her.

Stepping back into her space, she slides her arms around the back of my neck as I slip my hands under her ass and lift her into the air. I set her down on the kitchen counter, our mouths colliding once again. My hands move along her thin torso, feeling the curves of her toned body as I reach her breasts. Cupping them both in my hands, I roll her nipples between my fingertips as she wraps her legs around my waist.

Eden moans into my mouth and I swallow her sounds as she moves herself against me. I can feel the warmth of her pussy through her leggings, pressing against my waist. And I need to feel more of her. This isn't enough. I want all of her, right here, right now. Fuck going to her bedroom, fuck it if her roommate walks in.

I don't care.

I'm fucking intoxicated—drunk off Eden Finley —and I need to feel her now.

Abandoning her breasts, I slide my hands down to the waistband of her pants. She releases her legs from around my waist and lifts her ass into the air as I slide her leggings and panties down. Eden kicks off her shoes as I take a step back and begin to pull her clothes away from her feet. I toss them onto the floor, leaving her bare and spread out for me on the counter.

Eden stares back at me as my eyes scan her body, taking in the pure sight of her beauty. Her chest heaves, rising and falling with every shallow breath she takes. My heart pounds erratically in my chest and my cock throbs as I fight the urge to strip out of my clothes and dive deep inside her.

Stepping back into her space, I push her legs apart and drop down onto my knees in front of her. Grabbing her ass, I pull her closer to the edge of the counter, her legs draping over my shoulders.

"What are you doing?" she questions me, her voice completely breathless as her eyes search mine.

I stare back at her, the corners of my lips twitching. "I want to taste you, baby. Your attitude might be salty, but I have a feeling this pussy tastes sweeter than heaven."

Eden narrows her eyes at me before she slides her hands into my hair and pushes me closer to her. A grin pulls on the corners of my lips at her attempt to take control again. Spreading her legs wider, I dive in, sliding my tongue along her center as her fingers tangle in my locks.

A moan falls from her lips as I slide my hands under her ass, holding her in place as I run my tongue along her pussy. She tastes sweeter than anything I've ever tasted before. She might think that she's in control, but it's all a charade.

In this moment, she's mine.

And I plan on taking full advantage of that.

CHAPTER NINE
EDEN

My head is in the clouds with Hayden between my legs. My mind can't even process what he's doing with his tongue, but whatever it is, I don't want him to ever stop. He fucks me with his mouth, teasing my clit before licking my center. I can't hold myself up anymore, and my fingers slide out of his hair as I lay back on the countertop of the island in the kitchen.

The last thing I want is for Winter to come home and walk in on this, but I don't even care in this moment. Right now, all that matters is how close he's pushing me toward the edge. Hayden swirls his tongue around my clit, driving me crazy with every stroke. His hands grip my ass, his fingertips digging into my flesh, and I revel in the pain.

Pain mixes with pleasure and a warmth begins to spread through my body. My nails grip at the counter, but there's nothing for me to grab onto. Moans fall from my lips, over and over, as he continues to do wicked things to me with his tongue. He plays my pussy like a skilled musician and I can't take it anymore.

The euphoria is building and I can feel myself getting closer to the brink, to the edge of where I will fall into the bottomless pit of abyss. And I want nothing more from him right now. He continues to work his tongue against me and I can feel it. My orgasm hits me harder than I've ever felt before, tearing through my body like a goddamn hurricane.

It feels like I'm about to come apart at the seams.

"Oh god, Hayden," I moan, half crying out as my orgasm tears through my body. It's like a damn earthquake and I'm falling, floating as the ecstasy consumes my every thought. My nerve endings are on fire, my entire body tingling as the warmth spreads through my system like wildfire.

My legs shake, my hips bucking, but he doesn't move away from my pussy. He continues to work his tongue, licking and tasting every inch of me as my orgasm doesn't stop. I've never felt something so intense, and my body feels like I'm literally going to explode from what he's doing to me in this moment.

I'm still riding the high from him, my eyes rolling back in my head as he runs his tongue along my pussy once more. I feel his absence as he pulls away, his hands on my knees as he rises to his feet. My head feels like it weighs a ton and my vision is hazy as I lift my head to look up at him.

Hayden stares back at me with an indistinguishable look in his eyes. Emotion swims in his irises and he slowly pulls down his pants, pushing his boxers down with them. They pool around his feet on the floor and he steps out of them as he steps into my space.

"You're fucking beautiful, Eden," he murmurs, pushing my legs farther apart as the tip of his cock presses against my center. "And I promise you I've never said that to anyone else before."

Linking my legs around his waist, I pull him closer as he pushes his cock inside me. A moan falls from my lips as he fills me to the brim with one fluid movement. My body is still on fire, still tingling from the orgasm that he just brought me to. Feeling his thick length fill me has me seeing stars again.

"How do I know you're not just telling me what I want to hear?"

Hayden leans over me, sliding his hands over my torso until he slips his arms under mine and lifts me into a sitting position. He moves his hands back down to my ass, gripping my flesh as he holds me in place. My legs are wrapped around his waist and my hands find his shoulders as I cling onto him.

"Because that's not what you want to hear, Eden," he breathes, his face dipping closer to mine. "You want me to lie to you and tell you I've told all the other girls the same thing. You don't want to hear the truth because it makes you feel things you don't want to feel."

My breath catches in my throat, my heart pounding erratically in its cage as Hayden stares directly into my soul. His hands grip my ass as he slowly pulls out and thrusts back into me. My lips part, but words fail me. I feel completely exposed under his gaze, like he can see straight through me, down to my bare bones.

"Can I tell you a secret, baby?" he murmurs as he nips at my bottom lip and thrusts into me again.

Swallowing roughly, I nod. A moan escapes me as he fucks me gently, stroking my insides with his cock.

"I don't want to feel it either."

We can't go any further than this. I should stop

him right now, with the nonsense that he's talking, but he distracts me with his mouth as it collides with mine. His tongue swirls with mine, caught in a tangled dance as we move together.

He shifts his hips, his fingertips gripping my ass as he fucks me harder. He fucks the thoughts and feelings from my mind. All that is left is the physical feelings of him inside me, his hands on my body, and the way he's driving my body wild. That's all that matters in this moment.

Hayden thrusts into me harder and harder, pushing both of us closer to the edge. I can feel my orgasm building, playing against my nerves again as he strokes my insides. The tip of his cock hits my cervix over and over, the pain mixing with the pleasure. I'm so gone and lost in him. My nails dig into his skin as I hold on to him for dear life.

Abruptly, he stops, pulling out of me. His movements throw me off, my legs falling away from his body as he takes a step away. He slides his hands to my hips, lifting me off the counter and onto my feet. I stare up at him, a mix of confusion washing over my expression as my eyes search his.

"Turn around for me, baby," he murmurs, spinning me on my feet to face the counter. He inches me closer to it, the marble cold against my warm stomach as he presses me into it. His mouth finds the back of my neck, nipping at my skin before he trails his mouth down my spine as he presses the front of my body onto the counter.

"Are you on the pill?" he asks me out of nowhere. "You're the only one I've ever fucked raw before, and I don't want to feel you with any barriers if I don't have to."

Bent over at the waist, I glance at him over my shoulder. "Of course, I am. I am in no position to be getting pregnant right now."

"Good," Hayden growls as he lifts my feet off the floor and positions me on the counter. "I'm clean but I have every intention of dirtying you up."

His hands find my ass as he spreads my thighs with his own. He gives me no warning, abruptly thrusting his cock deep inside me. He fills me completely, a moan escaping me as I press my face against the cool marble.

"I'm gonna fuck you hard, Eden," he breathes, pounding into me again. "I'm gonna finally fuck you out of my system."

Glancing at him over my shoulder again, my gaze meets his and I don't miss the flames that burn in his irises. "Then stop talking about it and do it."

A shadow passes over his expression and he tightens his grip on my flesh as he shifts his hips. He pounds into me, harder with every thrust as he fucks me completely senseless. My head is swimming and I'm floating in the clouds, literally seeing the stars swirling around me. I can barely keep my eyes open as my orgasm continues to build, inching closer to the edge.

Hayden releases one of my ass cheeks and slides his hand around my front. His fingers instantly find my clit and he applies the right amount of pressure, rolling his fingertips over the sensitive bundle of nerves. That's all it takes to send me soaring over the edge of the cliff.

My pussy clenches, tightening around his length as my orgasm tears through my body. It literally feels like he's going to split me in two as he pounds into me harder, but I don't even care. He could literally tear me to pieces right now and it wouldn't even matter. His name falls from my lips as I struggle to catch my breath.

It's like an earthquake tearing through me, my entire body shaking as I shatter into a million pieces around him. He moves his hand away from me, grabbing my hips as he pounds into me once more before pulling out. I feel his warmth as he loses himself over my ass, coating me with his cum.

"Goddamn, Eden." His voice is husky and breathless. We're both riding out the highs of our orgasms and he pulls me away from the counter. My legs are shaky and unstable as I attempt to find my footing.

Instead of steadying me, he lifts me into his arms, not caring about his cum getting all over him. Neither of us pay any mind to our clothes that we left in the kitchen. I feel like I'm in a completely different universe with the euphoric state that he sent me into. My eyelids are heavy and I lay my head against his chest as he carries me through the apartment.

"Where's your bedroom, babe?"

I don't lift my head, listening to his heart pounding erratically in his chest as he cradles me like I weigh nothing. "Go down the other hall. It's the first door on the left."

My eyelids fall shut and his movements practically lull me to sleep as he carries me through the apartment and to my bedroom. He doesn't turn on the light as he enters and walks the two of us over to my bed. He pulls back the sheets before laying me down and covering me up.

Opening my eyes, I watch him as he hovers beside my bed before he goes to turn away. Reaching out, I grab ahold of his wrist and stop him. Hayden glances down at me, his eyes searching mine with an indistinguishable look in them.

"Stay with me?"

Hayden tilts his head to the side, inching closer to the bed, but he doesn't say anything.

"Just for the night," I whisper, pulling back the covers as I scoot over in bed to make room for him. "I can go back to hating you in the morning."

A smile tugs on the corners of his lips as he slides under the covers with me. He slips his arm underneath my neck, pulling me to him.

"Deal."

CHAPTER TEN
HAYDEN

"Oh my god, Hayden," Eden's voice is barely audible as she violently shakes me awake. "You need to wake the hell up."

Confusion washes over me and I slowly peel my eyelids open. The light shining through the window is harsh and I blink rapidly in an attempt to try and adjust. I'm still half asleep and Eden is practically shoving me out of her bed.

"What the fuck?"

Rolling over to face Eden, I take in her appearance. At some point, she slipped into a pair of sweatpants and a t-shirt. Her hair is in a messy bun on top of her head and she looks frustrated as hell. Her eyes are wide, her face flushed as she slices her gaze to mine.

"You need to go," she orders, shoving my shoulder again. "You're not supposed to be here. You weren't supposed to sleep here last night. Goddammit, Hayden. This isn't what was supposed to happen."

Narrowing my eyes, I raise an eyebrow at her. "So what? We fucked a few times and I fell asleep here. It's not a big deal." I pause for a moment, still confused by her urgency. "It's not like I asked you for forever. Shit, it was just one night."

"Yeah," she snorts, rolling her eyes as she points at the door. "One night, not a sleepover. Time to go."

"If I remember correctly, you're the one who told me to stay."

Eden doesn't like being called out and I watch the color drain from her face as the memory from last night hits her. I never once said anything about spending the night. She's the one who wanted me to stay, who insisted I get in her bed with her. She didn't protest when I fucked her into oblivion two more times after doing so in the kitchen. And when I finally fell asleep, she didn't wake me up.

"I never told you to spend the night with me." She glares at me, her frigid guard back up.

We're caught in an intense stare-down, her sitting on the bed and me still lying on my side with no intention of moving. It's clearly pissing her off and I have nothing better to do today.

"You never told me to leave either."

Her nostrils flare as she inhales deeply, closing her eyes in an attempt to calm herself. When she opens them, none of the anger has dissipated. Instead, she abruptly grabs the blankets and tears them from my body, leaving me fully exposed on her bed.

I can't stop the laughter as it falls from my lips. She's so pissed off right now and I can't help but find it amusing. And kind of cute.

"Shut up before Winter hears you," Eden orders, her voice low and cold as she grabs the pillow and pulls it out from under my head. Rolling onto my back, my chest vibrates as I continue to laugh, hearing the sounds of footsteps coming down the hall.

There's a soft knock on Eden's bedroom door and her eyes widen as she glances at me. "Eden," Winter's voice sounds through the door. "Are you alive in there?"

"Too late." I smirk.

Eden rises to her feet, her gaze trained on the

door as she slowly walks over to it. Winter knocks again, saying Eden's name with more panic in her voice. Slowly, I sit up on Eden's bed, grabbing the blanket from the floor as I cover the bottom half of my body with it. All of my clothes are still in the damn kitchen.

As Eden is about to reach the door, the knob turns and Winter pushes it open. Eden freezes a few feet away, her body rigid as she stares back at Winter. Winter tilts her head to the side, a mischievous look in her eyes as she glances back and forth between the two of us.

"Oh shit..." Her voice trails off for a moment. "I didn't realize you had someone in here."

Eden whips her head around, her eyes sending icicles through me. "He was just leaving."

Winter chuckles softly. "Well, he might need his clothes that he left in the kitchen." She glances at me over Eden's shoulder and winks. "I left them out there for you."

Fuck. As if this morning wasn't already off to a bad start, now I have to practically do the walk of shame through their apartment to get my damn clothes.

Fuck it.

Eden has already seen every inch of me,

completely naked for her. She wants me to go, then I'll make sure that I make a grand exit. Rising to my feet, I let the sheet fall away, dropping to the floor. I watch the horror on Eden's face as her cheeks turn pale and her eyes widen. Winter's eyes drop to my cock, nodding in approval.

"I'll show myself out," I tell the two of them, not bothering to cover myself up as I nod. My eyes find Eden's and if looks could kill, I'd be on the floor dead. "Call me next time you decide you want to make a bad decision again."

"I'm good. I think I got it all out of my system," she clips, her voice as frigid as her eyes as I stride past her. A grin tugs on the corner of my lips as Winter steps out of my way. I can feel both of their eyes on my back as I slip into the kitchen and grab my clothes. They're right on the floor where we left them last night.

I leave Eden's there as I pull on my boxers and pants. The sounds of their hushed voices float from her bedroom, but I can't make out a single word either of them is saying. Winter looked surprised at first, but then it was almost as if she was more amused than anything. I wonder what Eden has told her about me.

Grabbing my t-shirt and sweatshirt, I slip both

of them over my head. Reaching into the front pocket of my pants, I find my phone that I left in there last night and my keys. As I walk to the door, I can still hear Eden and Winter. As much as I want to eavesdrop, I let myself out of the apartment instead and leave the two of them in Eden's room.

The ride down the elevator feels like it takes forever and it makes it feel less like the walk of shame. Pulling out my phone, I check my messages and see a few from some of the guys. They were checking in, in our group chat to see where I was last night. I type a quick message, letting them know I'm on my way home, and don't give them any more details.

The less they know, the better. I don't want to hear the shit from any of them about me fucking around with Eden. They're afraid I'm going to hurt her and put her through hell after what she went through with her last relationship.

Little do they know, it won't be me who does the damage.

It will be Eden.

She might hate me, and that's okay, but that doesn't erase the fact that there's something inside her that melts when I'm around her. I'm not stupid or blind. I just don't know what to do with it except ignore it. Neither of us want a relationship, and I'm fine with that. We can stay enemies for as long as she wants.

As long as she keeps letting me fall into her bed.

CHAPTER ELEVEN
EDEN

"Don't start with me," I warn Winter, feeling the heat creeping up my neck before it spreads across my cheeks. She's standing back in the doorway that Hayden just disappeared through with a smirk on her face.

"I thought you went home last night because you were tired?" She raises an eyebrow with a look of amusement passing through her eyes. "How did Hayden King end up here?"

"I don't want to talk about it," I tell her, turning my back to her as I grab the sheet Hayden dropped on the floor before he made his dramatic exit. As if him being in my room wasn't embarrassing enough, he had to walk out completely naked for Winter to get a show. The sheet is still warm from his body and I position it back on my bed, slipping it under the comforter.

Winter sighs, ignoring me as she walks into my room and sits down on the papasan chair in the corner. "Nope. You aren't getting out of it that easily. You were able to keep your first encounter with him from me, but I just witnessed this shit with my own eyes." She crosses her arms over her chest in defiance. "Spill."

Closing my eyes, I run a frustrated hand down my face as I drop down onto my bed. An exasperated sigh escapes me as I lay my back down on the mattress. "Hayden showed up at the bar last night. You were talking to Travis, so you didn't notice him. He propositioned me for one last night and I agreed to it."

"Why didn't you just tell me then?"

Sitting up, I narrow my eyes at her. "Because I didn't want you to know. Shit, I don't want anyone to know about this. You know the reputation he has and I'm not about to have my name dragged through the mud because of him."

"Why are you so worried about what other people think?" she questions me, the curiosity heavy in her tone. There's no judgement, so I can't be mad at her for calling me out. "Usually, you don't care about what anyone thinks of you, except when it comes to Hayden."

"Because I don't want any association with him. He is the exact type of person I have tried so hard to avoid, yet I can't seem to get away from him. Everywhere I go, everywhere I turn, somehow he's always there."

Winter smirks. "And somehow he keeps ending up in your bed, huh?"

Grabbing the closest pillow to me, I chuck it at her from across the room. "It has only happened two times and will never happen again."

She catches the pillow and instead of throwing it back at me, she drops it onto her lap and stares at me for a moment. "Why? I mean, is he at least good in bed?" She pauses as she laughs. "I mean, I saw what your boy is packing. So please tell me he at least knows how to use it."

I can't fight the grin that tugs on the corners of my lips. Warmth spreads across my cheeks and I roll my eyes at her. "He's such an asshole. See, this is exactly why I can't stand him. He's so goddamn full of himself and cocky, like he's God's gift to everyone in the universe. Hayden King is untouchable, yet he can touch whoever he wants."

"Do I detect a little bit of jealously?"

Glaring at her, I purse my lips. "Absolutely not. I couldn't care less about what Hayden does or who he touches. I was simply just making an observation."

"Mhm," Winter mumbles, not fully believing my words. There's nothing I could possibly be jealous of. At the end of the day, I can't stand Hayden. Although, I haven't seen him with any other girls, even though I have seen them attempting to make advances toward him. It's kind of weird now that I think about it.

"So," Winter starts, interrupting my thoughts. "I don't need a play-by-play, but you never answered my question..."

Rolling my eyes, a smirk forms on my face. "Ugh. Yes, he knows how to use it and I think that's the problem. He knows that he's good in bed too, which only feeds his ego."

"You know, I don't see anything wrong with the whole situation," Winter shrugs with indifference. "No one said that either of you have to be friends, but clearly, he's into you. So, why not use that to your advantage? You don't have to be friends or in a relationship. Just let him relieve some of your stress occasionally."

"No way," I argue, shaking my head at her. "The

last thing I'm going to be with Hayden King is friends with benefits. We will never be friends."

Winter clicks her tongue. "Enemies with benefits?"

A sigh escapes me as drop back onto the bed again. I stare up at the ceiling with Winter's suggestion floating around in my head. "I can't believe I'm actually considering this."

"It sounds like the perfect thing, right?"

She isn't wrong. There's nothing that is binding Hayden and I together. We don't have to be friends; no one has to know about it. It would almost be like we're just helping each other scratch a mutual itch. Although, there is a part of me that thinks I would be better off just writing him off as it is.

I've slept with him two times—two times too many. He's someone I never should have gotten involved with, but I know there's no chance of ever developing feelings for him. Every girl in Hayden's life is disposable. He doesn't take anything seriously, except for himself and hockey. He's arrogant and cocky and gets on my damn nerves.

But I can't tell if it's all just a facade. I have yet to see the real Hayden King. The one that he keeps hidden from the rest of the world.

That's a place I can't even let my mind wander

to. I don't need to see or know that side of him because that's when things begin to get messy. When guards are let down and the ice around our hearts melts, how do we fight the fire that burns between us?

I'm not stupid or that naive. I know there's a connection between the two of us. There's something about him that keeps drawing me back in, even if I can't stand him. I can't let myself explore that, though. The last time I got involved with someone, I had my heart carelessly thrown back at me after it was torn into a million pieces.

And I refuse to let that happen again.

CHAPTER TWELVE
HAYDEN

As I walk into the locker room, most of the guys are already getting their gear on for practice. We have our first game this weekend and Coach has been on our asses about how we need to be better prepared. It was a rough start to the season with practices. There was almost a weird shift, as if none of us played with each other before.

Asher went back to Maine for the summer and played on a different league than the rest of us. Greyson and Liam both went back to their home-towns as well and played somewhere else. Not to mention the fact that we have five new freshmen on our team... it's been quite the adjustment.

They're all fairly decent players and there's a

reason why they all ended up at Wyncote. You don't come here to play on the team if you can't play hockey. And with a lot of us graduating at the end of this year, they need to bulk up their roster if they want to continue being on the top of the division.

The past two weeks have been pretty rigorous with practice. On and off ice, not to mention all of the lifting and workouts we've been having to do. I haven't heard from or seen Eden since that morning she kicked me out of her apartment, but that doesn't mean she hasn't been on my mind.

If I make it into the shower and am not completely exhausted, her face is what I picture while jerking myself off before crashing. I've literally been just trying to focus on my schoolwork and attending classes, and then the rest of my day is dedicated to hockey before I ultimately end up passing out for the night.

I'm not complaining. This is the life I signed up for and, to be honest, it's the only life I've known for a long time now. It's when I don't have anything going on with hockey that I tend to get myself into trouble. I need some type of a distraction when the boredom creeps in and it usually ends up going sideways.

Hockey helps keep my head on straight and my

life on track.

Although, there's a certain girl who's been invading the space in my mind. I thought I could fuck her out of my system and everything would be fine. I could go back to pretending like she didn't exist—but I was wrong.

It's beginning to feel more like I fucked her directly *into* my system instead of out.

I've wanted to reach out to her, but I don't have her number. I know where she lives and I'm sure she wouldn't appreciate it if I just dropped in on her. I can't come on too strong or I'll scare her away. Either that, or piss her off. Her distaste for me runs deep, but not deep enough for her to resist me when I'm near her.

"Am I the only one who really doesn't feel like doing this today?" Cam sounds out loud to no one in particular as he tightens his skates. I glance over at him as I strap on my shin pads and slide my socks over them. He looks as exhausted as the rest of us feel.

"No, I think we're all feeling it," August tells him, a sigh slipping from his lips as he shrugs on his practice jersey. "Today's the last practice before our game on Saturday, so we just have to get through this shit without Coach getting pissed."

Cam snorts and Simon rolls his eyes. "Easier said than done. With our luck, he'll probably make us come in to practice tomorrow too."

Vaughn Carter drops down onto the bench beside Cam. He's one of the freshmen and we've been doing our best to try and take them all under our wings. After all, once we leave, it's up to them to keep the legacy and team going. Simon Murray and Greyson Hale are all a year behind Logan, August, Asher, Cam, and I. So, the three of them will at least still be around until the new guys feel more comfortable here.

"Is this usually how it is?" Vaughn asks all of us as he slides the straps of his helmet on. "It seems pretty intense."

"Not usually," Logan tells him as he rises onto his skates and grabs his gloves and stick. "It depends on how everyone is playing. As long as we're doing what we're supposed to do, practice resumes as normal. Except when it's time for the playoffs. Then we're back to this shit."

August glances over at me as I finish getting dressed. "You're quiet today. You good?"

I look over at him as I rise to my feet and grab my gloves. Some of the guys are already heading out of the locker room and I wait until it's just August and me left in the room. I've known him for a long time now. August, Logan, Cam, and I all grew up together. The three of them came here for college, so we were separated for two and a half years.

But if there's anyone that I actually tell the inner layer of my secrets to, it's the three of them. Logan and Cam headed out before I had a chance to say anything and I know I can trust August and talk to them. We don't always see eye to eye on everything and I know he hasn't always agreed with the things I've done in the past, but that doesn't mean he doesn't have my back.

Especially after everything he went through himself. We all stuck by his side when he found out that Poppy was pregnant and they had to work things out between the two of them. Thank God they did and brought the most beautiful little boy into the world, whom we've all embraced as one of our own.

I honestly don't know how he does it and have to give him major props. Juggling school, a fiancée and baby at home, on top of our demanding schedule with hockey. He's gotta be fucking exhausted.

"I can't get this girl out of my head and I don't know what to do about it."

August raises an eyebrow at me. "You mean after all the shit you've talked about the rest of us settling down, you finally found someone who holds your attention for more than one night?"

I give him the middle finger before sliding my hands into my gloves. "I met her over the summer and we hooked up. I had no idea who she was until the school year started and I ran into her. She hates me, which is cool. It honestly makes shit hotter between us."

"You would be after someone who hates you," August chuckles, shaking his head. "Then again, I don't know if there's anyone who could possibly put up with your shit for long enough."

"You guys all stuck around," I remind him, winking.

August laughs again. "That's only because you're a kick-ass defenseman. We need you around." He pauses for a moment as we both grab our sticks and head out of the locker room. "So, who is she? And what's the problem?"

"I'm not at liberty to say who it is. And I don't know what the real problem is, honestly," I shrug as we walk down the tunnel toward the ice. "I ended up at her place, like, two weeks ago and haven't heard from her or seen her since."

August is silent for a moment, pausing by the door as I step out onto the ice before him. He's right behind me, our skates sliding across the icy surface as some of the guys skate past us. "You have her number or anything?"

I shake my head, grabbing a puck with my stick as I skate a circle around August. "I know where she lives."

"So, if you want to see her, go see her."

Tilting my head to the side, I slide to a stop as I raise an eyebrow at him. "Isn't that kind of a creeper thing to do?"

August steals the puck from me, laughing as he skates past me. "It's creepy enough that a girl has your attention for this long. If the shoe fits, fucking wear it."

His laughter follows after him and I can't help but laugh along with him. He's completely right. Eden's going to be pissed as shit when I show up at her front door, but I don't even care. I need to see her. You know, so we can fall in bed together once more and say that it's the last time even though we both know damn well it isn't.

I don't want anything more from her than that. And I think it's something we could come to a mutual agreement on. At least, I hope so.

Leaning down, I push off on one skate, repeating the motion with each foot as I power skate across the rink. My legs are sore from the intense week we've had and I'm honestly looking forward to the day off tomorrow. And as much as I want to go see Eden, it's going to have to wait.

I'm going to take August's advice, but not yet. I haven't run into her at the rink in the past two weeks, so I know she's been avoiding me. And I want to know why. I've hung around longer than I normally do, trying to catch her when they're supposed to be practicing. I don't know if she switched her schedule to skate at different times or what is going on.

This will have to wait until after the weekend. Eden is fucking with my head enough right now. I have to be on top of my shit this weekend at the game. Grabbing a puck, I skate around, stickhandling it before shooting it at Asher who blocks it from the net.

My future depends on how well I play. If I don't play well, our coach has no problem taking away ice time from people and that is the most important thing.

I'll deal with Eden Finley after the game.

At least I know I won't fuck the former up.

CHAPTER THIRTEEN
EDEN

Winter and I leave our apartment for the rink when the sun is just cresting the horizon. We were able to work it out with our coaches and the directors to give us time to practice in the morning. We've all been stuck working around the hockey team's schedule for years and for some of us, only being able to skate in the afternoons or evenings doesn't work. Especially when we have to do it when there isn't hockey practice.

There was no reason why they couldn't have the rink open to us in the mornings or during the day. So, I got Winter to come with me and convince them to let us. I didn't tell her that it was because I wanted to avoid any run-ins with Hayden. I just told her that I wanted other options and I like waking up and skating first thing in the morning.

My body isn't exhausted from the hours of the day before it and I feel like I personally skate better when it's the first thing I do. It helps to ease my soul and calm my mind. On the ice is the only place I truly feel at home.

As we pull up to the rink at campus, I notice there's only one car in the parking lot. A wave of relief floods me when I see that it isn't Hayden's black Subaru. I didn't think I would see him at the rink this early anyway, but it's only a matter of time before we run into one another again.

So far, I've been able to successfully avoid him. It's been a little over two weeks since Winter found him in my room and I kicked him out. I made the switch immediately for our skating sessions to be in the morning so I wouldn't chance seeing him when he was coming in for practice in the evenings.

I've contemplated what Winter suggested in my mind over the past few weeks and I still haven't made a decision on what I want to do. It seems like it could be a seamless plan, but I don't know if it's worth the risk. Once you start spending time with someone, it's hard to not fall into the habit of wanting to be around them even more.

And then one thing always leads to another, and then someone always ends up getting hurt. I know that Hayden and I have both expressed not wanting to be in a relationship, but how do you keep things strictly sexual with someone and not develop some type of feelings?

I can't let myself make the same mistakes I've made in the past. I learned my lesson the hard way with Chance and I refuse to go down that road again. Things with Hayden and I would never work out. And I can't help but wonder if it's better to go the safer route and just keep my distance from him. Hence why I've been avoiding every possibility of running into him.

Their team has been the talk of the week with the game that they played over the past weekend. From what I heard others talking about, they beat the other team effortlessly. It sounded like the other team didn't even stand a chance, which weirdly made me feel a sense of happiness for Hayden.

And that was a feeling I didn't like.

I would never wish anything ill upon him, or any of the other guys for that matter. At one point, I was really close with all of them. They always expressed their dreams of playing professionally one day and, to be honest, I want that to happen for each and every one of them.

But hearing that Hayden played such a great game and the fact that it made me happy for him threw me off. There's no place for any feelings for Hayden King in my life, whether it's happy or sad. I need to just keep my focus on the negatives where he is concerned.

"You okay?" Winter questions me as we walk into the empty arena and make our way to the locker room. None of the other girls wanted to come in this early and will probably be filing in when we'll be leaving for class.

Winter sits down on the bench and we both pull our skates out of our bags as we slip out of our sneakers. I look over at her and find her watchful gaze on my face. "Come on, Eden," she urges as she pushes her feet into her skates. "I can tell something's going on with you. You've been weird for the past few days."

I lace my skates up and rise to my feet as she does the same. "I just have a lot going on in my head right now."

"Hayden?" she asks with no judgement. My eyes meet hers and she frowns. "Have you seen him or talked to him since the other week?"

Shaking my head, we both walk out of the locker room and head down the tunnel toward the ice rink. "I've been trying to avoid him. You know how I feel about him and I don't know if it's worth getting involved with him, even if we keep it strictly sex."

"I mean, it's not like it's something you've done before," she says as we both step out onto the ice. "I get why the thought of it would freak you out. It's pretty simple if you don't let feelings get involved."

"And that's what I'm afraid is going to happen."

Winter spins on her skates and begins to move backward as she tilts her head to the side. "You're afraid you're going to develop feelings for Hayden? I thought you can't stand him?"

"I can't. But what happens if I get to know a different side of him and he works his way under my skin? Then what the hell am I supposed to do?"

"Would it really be such a bad thing?" she questions me before stretching out her legs on her skates. "I mean, I know you had a bad experience with a hockey player in the past, but that doesn't mean they're all the same way. Look at some of the other guys and the relationships they're in now."

I stare back at her for a moment. I know exactly what she's trying to say, but that changes nothing.

Nothing good would ever come from Hayden getting under my skin.

"That would be the absolute worst thing that could happen."

CHAPTER FOURTEEN
HAYDEN

After the way that we played last weekend, it was like Coach was lying the entire time. We came together as a team and we dominated. He's been going easier on us with practice now and we're back to only three times during the week with our games on the weekend.

I should have picked a different day to go see Eden, but whatever. There's no better time than the present, right? She throws me off-balance and I feel like I'm in uncharted territory. Usually, randomly showing up at a girl's house wouldn't be something I would question. Clearly, if she has something I want, I'm going to show up and collect.

It's different with Eden. I've played the scenario over in my head multiple times of how this could go.

And I only see two real options. Either she invites me in or she slams the door in my face. That is if she even opens the door when she sees that it's me.

Rolling my bag out of the rink, I pop my trunk as I walk across the parking lot. Most of the other guys are already pulling out onto the street, heading to the bar we frequent at. As I reach my car, I lift up my bag and shove it inside before putting my stick in with it.

"You coming out with us, King?" Simon asks me from where he stands by his car.

I shake my head. "I have something else I need to take care of."

He stares at me for a moment, looking like he wants to say something, but instead he clamps his mouth shut and shrugs. "All right. Well, I'll catch you later then."

A wave of guilt washes over me. Simon and I have grown pretty close over the past year and I've been keeping him in the dark about Eden. He knows what happened over the summer, but that's the extent of it. He made it clear that he didn't approve of me fucking around with her then, and I know his mind wouldn't have changed that easily.

I nod at him before making my way over to the driver's side. As I climb behind the wheel, I catch

August and Logan driving past and throw my hand up at the two of them. I'm not surprised when I see them turn in the opposite direction of all the other guys. Instead of going out, they have better things to do... like be with their fiancées.

———

The drive to Eden's apartment feels like it takes forever, even though it's only a short ride there. My heart pounds erratically as I pull into the parking lot and find a spot. I don't know what is going on. There aren't many things that make me feel nervous or unsure of myself, except for Eden.

Of course, I'll never let her know that.

It's easy to put on a facade and play a little charade with her. My confidence has never been a question and even though Eden makes me question it all, I've been fairly successful at keeping that from her. The last thing I need is for her to know the way she's been affecting me.

Walking through the darkness of the night, I can see my breath in the cold air. As I reach the front door to Eden's apartment building, my stomach sinks as I realize I can't even get inside past the small foyer. It's locked and the only way of reaching her is by pressing the button next to her apartment number on the wall and hoping she answers the intercom.

I'm thankful for the added security because it makes me feel better about her safety. But fuck...

Inhaling deeply, I turn toward the wall and find Eden's apartment number and press the small button beside it. It rings and I release it, shifting my weight nervously as I wait. It feels like an eternity, waiting for her, but the moment I hear her singsong voice float through the speaker, I swear my heart picks up speed.

"Yes?"

A ragged breath slips from my lips. I was afraid it was going to be Winter instead of Eden, if either of them decided to answer the ringing. Thankfully, it was Eden.

"Hey you."

She's silent for a moment. Anxiety races through my veins and I shift my weight again as I wait for her to say something. I can't help but feel like maybe she heard my voice and completely disappeared. I feel like a damn idiot standing here. I should have just been like a normal person and got her phone number instead.

"Hayden?" she practically whispers, and I can

hear the nervousness in her voice. "What are you doing here?"

A chuckle slips from my lips and I feel like I can breathe again. I wouldn't say that she sounds happy I'm here, but more shocked. And that's what I was going for, right? If she knew I wanted to see her, she would do everything in her power to make herself invisible from me. It's a little hard for her to do that now since I've already surprised her.

"I was in the area and thought I would stop by."

She's silent for another moment before her voice comes through the speaker, sliding across my eardrums like silk. "Did you want to come up?"

Shit. I let out a sigh, relief instantly flooding my body. When I came here, I knew there would be two things that'd happen. I just didn't fully expect her to really invite me in or want me to come up to her apartment again. I thought for sure I would get the opposite reaction from her.

I guess I really underestimated Eden. This is the kind of shit she does. Not only does she constantly challenge me and call me out on my bullshit, but she continues to surprise me. Just when I think I have her figured out, she goes and flips the script.

There's a lot about Eden Finley and how she operates that I don't know.

"I would love to," I admit, my voice sounding slightly breathless as I attempt to control my breathing and my heart that pounds erratically in my chest.

Eden doesn't say anything else and I wait for the sound of the door to unlock or something, but I suppose their apartment building doesn't have a mechanism like that. There's a sudden uneasiness inside me, a panicked feeling I don't like. No one gets under my skin or gets my guard down, except for this fucking girl.

And even though I'm not wearing my heart on my sleeve and spilling my deepest secrets to her, I'm still standing here, looking like a fucking fool. I wait for a few more moments, but she doesn't say anything through the speaker again. If she can't unlock the door from her room, then she has to come down here to let me in.

Shifting my weight, I peer through the door into the apartment building, looking for her, but I don't see her anywhere. I see the elevators over on the other side of the lobby, but it doesn't appear like they are moving. It's hard for me to really see from this angle and the darkness of the night. It doesn't look like the numbers are changing, though.

And in that moment, my heart sinks.

Eden Finley never liked me, but I would be lying if I said I didn't get my hopes up the moment she asked me to come up. I don't even know what I'm really here for. It seemed like a good idea, that I could show up and Eden would be down for anything, but what the hell was I really here for?

A good time, or something more?

Running a frustrated hand down my face, an exasperated sigh slips from my lips. It's a blow to my ego when I realize she isn't going to come down and let me in. And I can't say I blame her. Eden is smart and she knows what is good for her by keeping her distance from me. But that doesn't mean I don't want to eradicate that distance.

Jesus. Maybe I need to figure out what the hell I really want with her before I make a move. My thoughts are beginning to get muddled when it comes to her. I can't tell what is up or down anymore. It's beginning to feel like I'm ready to throw my ground rules out the window and I can't do that. I need to get my shit together before I get any closer to her.

Turning around, I walk through the small foyer area, reaching to push open the door that leads back outside. My hand reaches for the handle just as I hear something click. Glancing over my shoulder, I see the door pushing open and Eden ducks her head through the opening.

Her eyebrows tug together. "Where are you going?"

My breath catches in my throat and I swallow hard over the lump that lodges itself there. Turning around, I shove my hands into the front pockets of my pants. "I thought you were just fucking with me and weren't actually going to be coming down."

She stares at me for a moment. "You didn't like that thought very much, did you?"

Narrowing my eyes, I raise an eyebrow at her. "Did you purposely take your time coming down here just to see what I would do?"

She tilts her head to the side, her eyes staring directly into my soul. "Come on," she motions for me to follow her. "Let's go up to my apartment and you can tell me why you're really here."

I follow after her, into the apartment building. As we step onto the elevator, it takes everything in me not to press her up against the wall and claim her as mine. Instead, I keep my hands to myself. It's a silent ride up to her floor, but she leads me back to her apartment, tucking me inside with her.

It feels like the walls are closing in as she stares at me expectantly.

"Why are you here, Hayden?"

I swallow hard, that goddamn lump forming in my throat again. I can't stop the words as they free fall from my lips.

"Because I couldn't stay away."

CHAPTER FIFTEEN
EDEN

Standing in my kitchen, I stare back at Hayden, feeling the color draining from my face. It feels like my stomach is going to fall out of the bottom of my body as my heart beats against my rib cage. We're standing in the same kitchen where he laid me out on the counter and drove me past the point of oblivion.

Thankfully, Winter isn't here for the night. She went out with Travis and told me she wouldn't be home. She was planning on spending the night at his place, which is new for her, but I didn't question her on it. It seems like they're starting to get really close with one another and, to be honest, I'm really glad she isn't here since Hayden fucking King decided to drop by.

A shallow, ragged breath slips from my lips and I don't even bother attempting to hide the sound from him. He isn't putting his heart on the meat block for me to chop it, but he's giving me something that is more than he ever has before. Hayden is a sweet smooth talker. But the difference with him in this moment, is there's nothing charming about the way he's looking at me.

There's no playfulness in his tone. After the words came from his mouth, it looked almost as if they shocked him as much as they shocked me. Like he didn't plan on admitting that aloud, but once he spoke those words into the universe, they sucked every molecule of oxygen from the room.

"What?" I whisper, staring back at him as my eyebrows draw together. Hayden's eyes desperately search mine as he nervously runs a hand through his tousled hair. I've never seen him like this before and I don't like the way it's making me feel.

The butterflies in my stomach need to go back into hibernation.

"I know you've been avoiding me, Eden," he says quietly, tilting his head to the side as he slowly inches closer to me. I swallow hard as he enters my space, not stopping until the toes of his sneakers are touching the tips of my toes. "Tell me why."

"Because I don't like you," I practically choke out, the words tasting bitter on my tongue. "I have no reason to see you."

Hayden frowns, shaking his head as his eyes light up. His fingers are soft as he reaches out, brushing a piece of hair away from my face. "You can't bullshit a bullshitter, baby," he murmurs, his frown transforming into a smirk. "I'll give you three tries to tell me the truth."

"And if I don't?"

The corners of his lips lift higher, his smile shining in his eyes. "Then I'll just have to fuck the truth out of you."

My breath catches in my throat. My heart skips a beat before it takes off, speed racing inside my chest. Judging by the way he's looking at me right now, I know he's the only one in this room that is actually telling the truth.

"Tell me why you've been avoiding me."

Shit. I stare back at him for a moment, attempting to get my heart under control before it bursts through my rib cage. I don't want to tell him the truth, but it's either that or he follows through on his promise. But I'm not sure the latter sounds like that bad of an idea.

"Because you make me feel things that I swore I

would never let myself feel again," I admit, instantly regretting it as I watch the playfulness disappear from his expression. "You're only going to hurt me in the end, and I can't let that happen."

Hayden's eyebrows draw together and he winces, almost as if I metaphorically slapped him. "Why do you think that?"

"That's what guys like you do, Hayden," I tell him, shaking my head as I take a step back to put some distance between us. It doesn't make a difference. I can't breathe any easier even with the space. It still feels as if he's suffocating me and I don't like being cornered like this. "You find someone that catches your attention and once you get bored with them, you toss them to the side."

Hayden looks genuinely confused as he falls silent for a moment. "I thought you hated me, Eden."

"I do," I say in a rush, watching his face as he winces again. His throat bobs as he swallows roughly, but he doesn't interject and gives me an opportunity to correct my words. "I did. I don't know what I feel anymore when it comes to you, Hayden. And that's what I don't like. It was easier when I knew I hated you and everything that you represented. Now, I just don't know."

"So, don't let your feelings get involved," he says matter-of-factly, as if it's something I have control over. "We don't have to let our feelings dictate what happens between us. I came here because I can't get you out of my head. I tried to stay away and I couldn't anymore. That doesn't mean I want a relationship or it has to be any more than what it is. Stop overthinking shit and just let it be whatever it is."

My eyes bounce back and forth between his. What he says sounds pretty similar to what Winter had proposed. The only option I saw when it came to Hayden. But for some reason, now it just doesn't feel right and maybe it's because he's the one suggesting it. I wanted to present the idea to him but instead, he beat me to it.

"What is this then?"

Hayden's jaw tics and he shakes his head. "No, Eden. No labels. It's just whatever we want it to be in the moment."

"I don't want to be your friend," I tell him, my voice catching in my throat as he steps back into my space. I take a step backward and he continues to follow me.

"I never said I wanted to be your friend," he

smirks with a sinister look in his eyes. "I just want the benefits."

My lower back brushes against the edge of the counter as Hayden corners me. "Enemies with benefits."

"Whatever you need to call it to make yourself feel better," he murmurs, as he slides his warm palm along the side of my face. His touch is gentle as he strokes my skin with his fingertips. "Just as long as you're admitting that you feel it too."

Inhaling deeply, I let my eyelids fall shut, breathing in the scent of him. He smells of fresh soap, like he just stepped out of the shower. Which actually makes sense, considering his damp hair. He must have gotten finished at practice and showered before coming straight here.

"I feel it," I whisper, opening my eyes as I tilt my head back to find his gaze. "And I don't want to."

"Then don't feel anything other than this moment between us. What happened before and what happens in the future doesn't even matter. What matters is this single moment in time."

The words are on the tip of my tongue. I want to ask him what happens when this becomes some-thing more, when I start to fall for him. As much as I've tried to focus on my hate for him, there's been something else happening with my feelings for him, and I can't. I just cannot fucking go there.

"Get out of your head, baby," he breathes, his eyes bouncing back and forth between mine. "Stop overthinking and just be here with me."

"I don't know if I can," I admit, shaking my head. Ducking away from his hand, I move away from the counter, freeing myself from the cage he created around me. "This is a terrible idea, Hayden. And I'm not sure this is a mistake I want to make."

The ghost of a smirk plays on his lips. "Did you learn from your mistakes with me?"

Swallowing roughly, I nod. "We can't do this."

"Says who?"

My eyes slice to his as I cross my arms over my chest. "Me."

Hayden moves away from where he has been standing, closing the space between us once more. "What if I told you I wouldn't hurt you?"

"Then you'd be lying?"

He raises an eyebrow at me. "Do you really want the truth from me, Eden? Do you want me to bury my secrets inside you? Or do you want to take this all at face value so you don't get hurt then?"

His words surprise me. Everyone wants the truth, but in this moment, the thought scares me.

There's something Hayden isn't telling me and if it's the truth, then I don't think I want it. The air crackles from the electricity between us, the intensity something I've never felt before.

He's already admitted that he couldn't stay away. He's said in the past about how he needed to fuck me out of his system, and it didn't work.

Hayden King is fucking with my head.

And I'm not sure I want him to stop.

As long as my heart doesn't get involved...

CHAPTER SIXTEEN
HAYDEN

I can't tell her the truth. She doesn't want to get hurt and I don't want to hurt her. If she knows my truth—the real feelings I've been feeling—it will only make things worse between us and more complicated. Neither of us want to do complicated. Hell, neither of us want to do more than what we've been doing.

So, why the hell do our hearts have to go and betray us and get involved?

Eden is already under my skin, burrowing herself into my soul. She just doesn't know it and I don't intend on ever revealing that truth. As long as I can have her to myself, that's enough for me. I don't do relationships and she's the last person that I want to let down.

And I have a hard time believing that I will live up to her expectations.

She already has a thing against hockey players, after what her ex did to her. I would never do the same to her, but I can't expect her to follow me wherever I go after graduation. That's not fair to her and I'm not going to be the one who ruins either of our dreams.

Instead, I'm putting my feelings aside and trying to just enjoy this period of time with her, however long it might last. I just need Eden on the same page, or else it won't work. She keeps reiterating that she doesn't like me and it's becoming quite amusing.

I can't tell who she's trying to convince of that anymore, because her actions tell me a hell of a lot more than her words do. And it's quite a contradiction.

"I don't want the truth from you," she whispers as she tilts her head back to look up at me. Sliding my hand around the back of her neck, I stare down into her eyes. "I just want this. The simplicity and the ease of it all. Nothing more."

"Whatever you want, baby," I murmur, dropping my face down to hers. "You can pretend to hate me all you want, but when you're with me, you're mine."

She tilts her head to the side, her lips brushing against mine. "And what if I'm with someone else?"

I can't fight the growl that rumbles in my chest as I tighten my hand on the back of her neck. "We may not be anything more than this, but there's no one else. You got that?"

There's a crack in the ice that keeps Eden safe. "I expect the same from you then."

A chuckle slips from my lips. "Oh, baby, baby, baby," I breathe, nipping at her bottom lip. "Since I followed you to your tent that night, I haven't been able to get you out of my mind."

Eden wraps her arms around the back of my neck, lifting herself up onto her tiptoes as our mouths collide. She doesn't want to hear the truth from me, so instead I'll give her half-truths. Even though I may have slept with a few girls since that first night with Eden, that doesn't mean there has really been anyone but her. She's always been lingering in the back of my mind, burrowing herself under my skin.

This girl has a hold on me that she doesn't even know about and I refuse to admit it out loud.

Sliding my hand around the back of her head,

my fingers slide through her silky strands as I slide my tongue along hers. Caught in a delicate dance, they tangle with one another as I slide my other hand down to her hip. Pulling on her, I tug her closer until our bodies are flush against one another's. Eden holds on to me for support as our lips mold together.

Nothing matters in this moment except this. This is all that I want. She is all that I want.

Releasing her head, I slide my other hand down to her hips and move both under her ass. Lifting her into the air, she gasps against my mouth as she instinctively wraps her legs around my waist. As appealing as fucking her in the kitchen is, I want her spread out for me on her bed. To worship and thoroughly enjoy.

My feet carry us through the apartment until I find my way through the dark, carrying her into her bedroom. I don't bother shutting the door and Eden doesn't say anything. Instead, her mouth finds my neck, sucking and nipping at my skin. My cock strains against my pants and she's driving me mad with the way she slides her tongue along my flesh.

Lowering her down onto the bed, I slide my hands out from under her ass as I lay her down. Her arms are still linked around the back of my neck, pulling me down with her. Her head hits the mattress, her hair spreading out across the comforter like a halo around her head. Reaching up to grab her hands, I pull them away from me as I rock back onto my knees.

Eden stares up at me, her hands falling onto her chest. My gaze trails over her body, watching the way her rib cage expands and contracts with every breath she takes. Pressing my fingertips against her collarbone, I slowly drag them along her torso, feeling the planes and curves of her body through her clothes.

She slowly releases her legs from around my waist, her feet falling onto the mattress as she moves her hips. Lifting them into the air, she attempts to get close to me. My hand reaches for her waist, pushing her ass back against the bed. Eden moans in protest, a fire burning in her gaze as it collides with mine.

"Please, Hayden," she breathes, her pulse visible in her throat. Leaning forward, I press my mouth to the exact spot, feeling her blood pumping as her heart races in her chest. A smile pulls on my lips as I slide my tongue along her skin, dragging it down the column of her throat.

"Patience, baby," I murmur against her flesh

before biting at it. I run my tongue along the half-moon shapes that I leave in her skin. "Good things come to those who wait."

"Well, I've been waiting a long fucking time since the last time you were here."

Lifting my head up, a smile crooks on my lips as I raise any eyebrow at her. "If I remember correctly, you're the one who kicked me out that morning."

She lifts her finger and presses it to my lips as she hooks one hand around the back of my neck. "Shhh," she murmurs, shaking her head at me. "I like it better when you don't talk."

"And why is that?"

Eden rolls her hips, her eyes fluttering as she inhales deeply. "Because you always say the right things."

A chuckle slips from my lips as I press them back to hers. I let Eden take control, sliding her hands under my shirt as her mouth moves against mine. She pushes me back and I let her pull off my shirt as she sits up with me.

She doesn't wait for me to make a move and removes her own shirt and bra before I even have the chance to. I love her energy and the fact that she doesn't fuck around. Eden gets straight to the point.

And if this is all she's going to give me, then I'm going to take everything I can get.

I move off the bed, watching her as she removes her pants and underwear and tosses them to the floor. I'm still dressed from the waist down, but my cock is as hard as a fucking rock as I take in the sight of her. Spread out, naked for me on the bed... exactly where I want her.

My throat constricts and it feels like a vise grip tightens around my heart. I'm suddenly overcome with an emotion that I don't dare put a name to. Swallowing hard over the lump in my throat, my eyes meet Eden's. She stares at me, with no judgement or hesitation. She's ready to dive into the waters, regardless of where the current might drag us.

I know this is a mistake, and I can't stop myself from making it with her.

She was right about how this will end, yet I still can't stop this from happening.

Sliding my hands under the waistband of my sweatpants, I push them and my boxer briefs down before stepping out of them. Eden doesn't tear her gaze from mine, watching me as I climb onto the bed and over the top of her. Her lips part slightly, a ragged breath slipping from her. She's an enigma. The mystery girl that I met at the lake.

So fucking ethereal, yet so fucking deadly.

Planting my hands on the bed, on either side of her head, I settle between her thighs. She spreads them and wraps her legs around my waist as I shift my hips, slowly pressing into her. A moan falls from her lips, her gaze still on mine, and I feel that damn vise grip tightening in my chest again. I need to push her out of my mind, forget that it's her and just get lost in the moment.

But I can't...

I can't get lost in the moment, because I'm already lost in her.

CHAPTER SEVENTEEN
EDEN

Rolling over in bed, I feel his warmth before I even open my eyes. Neither of us talked about him spending the night with me, but after we were fully satiated and he slipped under the covers with me, I couldn't make him leave. There's something about him that makes me feel safe and having his arms wrapped around me put me to sleep in no time.

We keep making these same mistakes and it's only a matter of time before it's going to come back to bite one of us in the ass. With the way Hayden is able to disconnect, I have a feeling it's going to be me that will get bit.

And then I'll be left with a hole in my chest, in the shape of Hayden King.

I want things to be simple between us, with no complications. When it ends, it ends. No lingering feelings or repercussions from our actions together. It's all easier said than done. I didn't want Hayden to work his way under my skin, but it's too late.

He's already there.

He's been there longer than I've realized or wanted to admit. If he would have just let things go after that first time over the summer, I wouldn't be having this damn problem with him. I need to follow his instructions, though. Just stop overthinking. Don't put more thought into this and make it something it's not. Just take it for what it is—whatever the hell that is.

I'll just live in my own little fantasy world until the inevitable happens and I watch everything crumble around my feet.

Hayden's eyes are closed and he snores lightly. The room is bright from the sunlight that shines in through the windows. My eyes scan his face, taking in the innocence that isn't usually visible. There's something about his expression like this, almost as if his guard is down and there's a way for me to slip inside. To get a look at the real Hayden King, not the facade he presents to the rest of the world.

Something shifted between us last night. Even

though we both decided to keep this strictly physical, I can't help but feel like we've transitioned into a deeper connection. He made it clear that I'm not allowed to see anyone else as long as this is going between us. That was never my intention anyway, but I needed him to know that the same applies to him.

Even if we don't have a label, there still needs to be some type of exclusivity with us. I've never been good at sharing and I'm not about to put myself in that type of situation.

Thankfully, Hayden agreed. It's hard to tell what is the truth or not with him and that's mainly my fault. He's never given me a reason to not trust him, but I've been burned before in the past. A scorned woman will always be on the defense, looking for a reason to run in the opposite direction.

I can't let my emotions get the best of me and cloud my mind. There's nothing wrong with enjoying a good time, even if it happens to be with the one guy I despise. Which is another problem I'm beginning to struggle with. Perhaps I've been too harsh on him. I marked him as guilty by association without even knowing him. I made a judgement and had refused to see anything else.

But with this shift... I'm currently questioning everything.

"What are you thinking about, pretty girl?" Hayden murmurs with his eyes still closed. He startles me as he speaks, since I was convinced he was still asleep. His eyelids lift, revealing his green eyes. "I want to know what is going on inside that beautiful mind."

My breath catches in my throat as I feel completely exposed under his gaze. "It's relatively boring in there," I choke out, attempting to dismiss the way he makes my heart flutter.

"I refuse to believe that," he whispers, his voice barely audible. "There's not a single boring thing about you, Eden Finley."

Hearing him whisper my name might be my favorite sound.

"How did you sleep?" he questions me, changing the subject as he throws me off again.

"Good. How about you?"

His lips curl upward. "Better than I normally do."

My heart keeps trying to crawl into my throat and I keep swallowing it back down. We both fall into a silence that once would have been comfortable, but now under his watchful gaze, I feel entirely too exposed. Sliding out from under the covers, I grab my clothes and quickly put them on. As I turn back around to face Hayden, he's still comfortable on the bed with a look of amusement on his face.

"Running away so soon?"

Clearing my throat, I shake my head as I move across the bedroom. "I need to go to the bathroom."

Hayden nods, but falls silent, his gaze following me as I quickly shuffle out of the bedroom. As I walk out into the hall, I hear the sound of music coming from the kitchen and the smell of coffee. My stomach sinks as I realize that Winter must have come home early this morning.

Which means she knows that Hayden is here... again.

Thankfully, the bathroom is at the opposite end of the hall, so I'm able to slip inside without chancing a run-in with Winter. As I enter, I shut it and lock it before using the bathroom. After washing my hands, I make sure to brush my teeth twice before splashing my face a few times with cold water.

Grabbing a spare toothbrush from the cabinet, I set it on the counter for Hayden. I glance at myself in the mirror, wincing at how I look. I'm not usually one who is overly concerned with my looks, but I can't help but feel slightly self-conscious knowing Hayden saw how I looked waking up. Pulling my hair on the top of my head, I wrap my hair tie around it and secure my locks in a messy bun.

It's not much better than how it looked before, but it's better than the tangled mess that was hanging around my face.

As I unlock the bathroom door, I slowly turn the knob and pull it open, careful to not make too much noise. Keeping my footsteps light, I go to step into the hall and gasp as I almost run into Winter.

She's standing just outside the door, a smirk on her face as she leans against the wall. Her eyes meet mine and I notice the curiosity and mischief mixing in her irises.

"Good morning," she says sweetly, offering me a genuine smile. "You look like you had quite the night."

My breath catches in my throat, coming out as a strangled choking sound as I attempt to recover from her surprising me. "I didn't think you would be home already."

Winter shrugs, her face falling for a moment, but she's quick to put her poker face back in place. "Travis and I had a little disagreement, so I left first thing in the morning. That shit is most definitely done."

"Why?" I question her, the sympathy laced in my words. They really seemed like they were getting along and hitting things off. I'm surprised to hear she's writing him off already. "What happened?"

"Nothing worth giving any more attention," she admits, sighing. "He's not the guy I thought he was. I mean, he's still nice and a great guy, just not the one for me. We got into an argument over moving away from here. You know that I love Vermont, and he absolutely hates it. Girl, you know I would melt if I lived anywhere other than here. It's just not worth putting any effort into building something with someone who's going to leave in the end."

I frown, her words hanging heavily in my head and the weight of them drags me back to where my mind keeps drifting to Hayden. "I completely get that. And good for you, I don't blame you. I'm all for living in the moment, but life is too short to waste your time with someone you might not have a future with."

The corners of Winters lips lift upward. "So, I'm guessing that you decided Hayden King is worth your time then?"

Pulling my lips in between my teeth, I bite down

as I inhale deeply. Closing my eyes, I shake my head and swallow hard over the lump in my throat. As I lift my eyelids, I meet Winter's gaze, which is now filled with concern. Her eyes bounce back and forth between mine, searching them for an answer.

"I don't know what I'm doing with him," I tell her, my voice barely audible. I don't like admitting it out loud and instantly want to take the words back. "We talked last night. It's nothing different than it was before. We're just going with whatever it is and not getting involved with anyone else."

"So, you're exclusive to each other without any labels?" She shakes her head, flashing her white teeth at me as she pushes off the wall. "Let me know how long that lasts for you guys." She chuckles. "It's only a matter of time before he's wifing you up."

My eyes widen and my heart pounds rapidly in my chest. "Oh no, that is not happening."

"I'm calling it now."

"I hate to interrupt, but can I use the bathroom?" Hayden's voice comes from the doorway of my bedroom as he pokes his head out. "I don't mean to be graphic, but if I wait any longer, my bladder might explode."

Winter's face lights up as she chokes out a laugh. "I'll leave the two of you to it." She winks at me before turning around to head down the wall. She passes Hayden, flashing a smile at him. "Nice to see you, Hayden. And thanks for not leaving your clothes in my kitchen."

I watch her disappear as Hayden strides toward me, fully dressed in the outfit he wore here last night. His eyes are bright and meet mine as he flashes his expensive smile at me.

"I left a toothbrush on the counter for you," I tell him, stepping out of the way for him to go into the bathroom.

He tilts his head to the side, raising an eyebrow at me. "Shit, I have my own toothbrush here now? Damn, baby, I didn't know we were moving that fast."

Rolling my eyes, I brush past him, intentionally shoving my shoulder into his. "Shut up, King. It's a toothbrush, not a ring."

I hear him chuckling from behind me as he slips into the bathroom. Leaving him to it, I walk into my bedroom and sit down on the edge of my bed. An exasperated sigh slips from my lips as I fall onto my back with my hands over my head.

What the hell did I get myself into?

CHAPTER EIGHTEEN
HAYDEN

I tried not to listen to Eden and her friend's conversation the other morning, but it was hard not to. Surprisingly, she didn't kick me out like she did the previous time. I was the one who had to cut out early, though. I had classes I needed to get to and she had some afternoon ones. That was two days ago, and now here I am, getting ready to go to one of her competitions.

She didn't officially invite me, but she mentioned it being at one of the local rinks tonight. It's open to the public to attend, so I figured I would see her in action and go to show my support.

Although, she has no idea I'm coming, so it's going to be a complete surprise. And I don't intend on letting my presence being known until after she finishes. The last thing I want to do is mess up her routine.

"Whoa, whoa," Simon sits up from where he was lying on the couch. "Hayden King, wearing something other than sweatpants and a hoodie or his jersey?"

Rolling my eyes, I stride past the couch and partially ignore Simon's comment. Yeah, I don't usually wear jeans, but it felt like a special occasion tonight to actually dress like a normal member of society.

"Where are you off to all dressed up?" Sterling questions me from where he's sitting at the island in the kitchen, shoveling spoonfuls of cereal into his mouth.

"You guys are ridiculous. I'm not dressed up."

"I mean, Simon wasn't lying. I don't know if I've ever seen you in a pair of jeans. Maybe a suit before a game, but this is definitely different," Sterling says, with an unusual bite to his tone. He's given me a lot of shit about Eden, so I've made sure not to share anything with either of them.

But you know what, fuck it. She's going to be around, so I'm done hiding it all.

"Eden has a competition tonight, so I'm going to go show my support."

Sterling raises an eyebrow but doesn't offer anything in response.

"Good luck, man," Simon offers from where he's sitting on the couch.

I turn around to look at him. "With what?"

"With Eden," he says matter-of-factly with a shrug. "I know how you are and I've never seen you this persistent with another girl before. I can tell it's different. Just do us all a favor and don't hurt her."

His words are like a knife to my chest. "I don't plan on it."

"That's funny," Sterling chimes in, his voice harsh. "Orion said the same thing."

My eyes slice to his. "Well, it's a good fucking thing that I'm not him."

Sterling stares at me for a moment, falling silent as his face softens. "I'm not trying to be an asshole. I just don't want to see her get hurt again. Eden has been so closed off to everyone, only worrying about herself. And if she's letting you in, that means something. You're melting her ice and I'm afraid what that will do to her if something happens."

"Eden can take care of herself," I tell him, my words clipped. "I have no intentions of hurting her, but regardless of what happens between us, she can handle more than you give her credit for."

"You're right," Sterling admits, backing down. "What happens between the two of you isn't anyone's business but your own."

"Thanks." I nod, not sure if I fully believe him, but whatever. "I don't know when I'll be back tonight, so I'll probably just see you guys before the game tomorrow."

"Sounds good," Simon calls out from the living room.

I glance over at Sterling and he nods before turning his attention back to his phone. A sigh slips from my lips before I slip out of our house. I should have just kept my apartment when I first moved here. I grew close with the guys from the team and when those two asked me to rent a house with them, I was completely in.

And now, I'm really regretting it.

Heading into the driveway, I climb into my car and turn on the engine, letting it idle for a moment before pulling out onto the street. I understand Sterling and Simon's concern and wanting the best for Eden. They all used to be close and they've known her longer. I totally get it. But at the same time, I wish for once that everyone would stop expecting the worst from me.

It feels like it's been that way my entire life. My

parents supported me playing hockey, but my father always expected the worst from me. I didn't want to follow in his footsteps and he didn't approve of that. He still supported me trying to shoot for the stars, but he made his disappointment clear.

All of the times I fucked up throughout life, it was like I was the black sheep of the family. My sister was the one who made them proud, even though I had something I was amazing at. It was never enough, so at some point I said fuck it. They expected me to fuck up, so that's what I started doing.

Except when it came to hockey. That was the one thing I had, and I refused to ruin something good like that. And my father expected that to blow up in my face eventually too. I'm sure he still thinks I'm going to fuck it up one day, but I can't let that happen.

There has to be something good in my life and that's always been hockey.

Until I met Eden Finley...

———

The parking lot is more crowded than I anticipated as I pull up to the rink. Given that we live in a northern state, figure skating is big, but nothing really comes close to touching the popularity of hockey. I'm a little surprised at just how many people are here to watch the competition.

Unless, it's a bigger event than Eden let on. She hasn't talked to me about it much, even though I know she's one of the biggest figure skaters in the area. I just didn't realize the caliber of the competitions she skates in.

When I walk into the arena, it's completely packed with people. As I walk over to the stands, I glance out at the rink, watching as all of the skaters are sliding across the ice, practicing their routines. I have no idea when Eden is expected to perform, but I'll sit here as long as I have to just to watch her skate.

I finally find a seat toward the top of the stands, but it gives me a decent view of the rink. Scanning the ice below, I see Winter working by herself. As my gaze moves over to the other side, I spot Eden as she lifts into the air, spinning, before she effortlessly lands on the ice again. My breath catches in my throat at how graceful she looks.

Absolutely fucking beautiful.

She's captivating and breathtaking—quite literally.

It takes everything in me to not go down to her, but I'm literally mesmerized as I watch her continue to move across the ice. She's lost in the moment, in her own head, as she focuses solely on what she's doing.

I know the guys have mentioned before that Eden only cares about Eden, but I've seen a different side of her. She's not who they portrayed her as, and maybe that's just the side of her they know of after her nasty breakup. She's clearly dedicated and committed to her sport, but that's no different than the rest of us.

The skaters clear the ice and the Zamboni comes out to clean the rink as they all get changed for their routines. After the ice is cleaned off, they announce the first skater who I'm not familiar with. The announcer says that she's from Wyncote, but her name doesn't ring a bell.

I watch as she skates around the rink, her performance mediocre, I suppose. If I'm being completely honest, I'm fairly ignorant when it comes to figure skating. I've seen them at the rink on campus, but other than that, I've only ever caught small bits of it from watching the Winter Olympic Games.

The next few skaters complete their performances, one of them being Winter. She scored decent and according to the announcer, she's sitting in second place. I watch the next few go out too, but none of them manage to knock Winter out of her place. A smile touches my lips, as I'm silently rooting for my girl's best friend.

A lump forms in my throat at the thought. My girl? Is she, though? Not officially. I mean, I don't really know. This entire thing is a mindfuck, but I know she's no one else's but mine, and that's all that matters.

The announcer's voice comes back through the speakers and my heart pounds against my rib cage as I hear Eden Finley's name being announced. Scooting to the edge of my seat, I sit up straight with my eyes glued to the ice as she steps out. She looks like she was made for a pair of skates as she effortlessly moves around the rink before stopping in the center.

She gets into a form that resembles a dancer's, her head bowed as music begins to play through the speakers. My heart pounds harder in my chest as I know the classical melody. "River Flows in You" by Yiruma. The only reason I know the song is because my sister played piano and when she went through her *Twilight*-obsessed phase, she constantly played this song.

Eden lifts her head as the melody picks up, her skates sliding across the ice in an angelic way, almost as if she's floating. The bottom of her dress-like outfit floats around her as she crosses her skates over, spinning around backward. She goes into some type of form, spinning rapidly in one place as she lifts her leg behind her head, her hands reaching the bottom of her skate as she lifts it higher.

I wish I paid attention when my sister did ballet, because it looks like one of their moves and I have no idea what it's called. It doesn't even matter at this point, because I am entirely captivated by the way she moves, regardless of what the fucking names are.

She spins faster, releasing her leg as she straightens her body into a straight line. Her body shifts, bringing her leg in front of her as she bends her knee and half crouches. I've never witnessed something so graceful, it's like watching moving art.

As she comes to a slower speed, she rises back up and begins to skate again, floating across the ice. She shifts her body again, skating backward as she continues to cross her legs over. I watch in awe as her legs move faster, her muscles tightening as she takes a turn backward, gearing herself up for something.

It's almost as if she grows a pair of wings. Bending her knee slightly, she pushes off with one leg, soaring through the air as her body spins. My mouth falls open and it's like the oxygen is stolen from my lungs as I watch her land her move with one skate touching the ice. Her other leg is stretched out behind her before she brings it back with the other. I'm no judge, but the entire thing looked flawless.

There's no hesitation in her moves, the confidence radiating off her, and I can feel it in the air from where I'm sitting. She doesn't give a shit about anyone in this arena right now. The only thing that matters right now is Eden and the ice.

She finishes the rest of her performance, throwing in one more jump spin move thing. I watch her as the song comes to an end, the melody slowing down. Her movements are slower, but the precision is still there. Pure fucking majestic art.

Eden comes to a stop in the center of the rink, ending her routine with her body dropping to the ice and her chin tucked to her chest. The entire building falls silent for a few moments before people begin to applaud. Tears prick the corners of my eyes and I can't even name the emotions that tear through my body right now.

I've literally never witnessed something this beautiful before. Rising to my feet, I clap loudly, feeling the moisture of my tears as they fall from my eyes. I don't give a shit that people are staring at me, considering I'm the only one standing. Nothing matters in this moment except for Eden and her moment.

She curtseys before spinning to the other side of the rink and doing the same, offering a wave. Wiping the tears away from my face, I take my seat and watch her as she skates to the door and steps out of the rink. The arena falls silent again as the announcer's voice comes back through the speaker.

Eden moves into first place with her flawless performance.

And the rink isn't the only place she moves into first...

CHAPTER NINETEEN
EDEN

I'm exhausted after the long night. Although I only had one performance, it still takes so much out of you. It's demanding on your body and the focus it requires. Tonight has been one of my best nights skating. The Lutz is definitely one of my signature moves, but I really killed it tonight.

After coming in first place, it was just as exhausting in the locker room. All of the other skaters from Wyncote gushed about how well I did. The only thing I wanted to do at this point was just go back to my apartment and crawl into bed after a nice long, hot shower.

The air outside is cold as I step into the parking lot. Wrapping my coat around my body tighter, I attempt to hold in some of my body heat as I make my way to my car. Winter was going out with some of the girls tonight, so she was just going to get an Uber back to our apartment. I'm too tired to even think about going out right now.

As I make my way to my car, my heart climbs into my throat as I see Hayden leaning against his car that is parked next to mine. He sees me as I walk toward him and pushes off the front hood with a smile on his face and a bouquet of flowers in his hand.

I walk over to him, meeting him a few feet away from our cars. His eyes shine under the lights in the parking lot as he smiles down at me.

"These are for you," he says, his voice soft as he hands the flowers to me. "After that performance, you deserve thousands of flowers, but this was all I had on hand."

Looking down at them, a smile touches my lips as I take them and hold them to my chest. "Thank you, Hayden." I pause for a moment, tilting my head to the side. "You came to watch?"

A shyness takes over his expression and it melts my heart. "I hope you don't mind. You mentioned it the other day and I wanted to see you in action, but I didn't want to surprise you before you went out on the ice."

I feel my guard dropping slightly from his words alone. Not only his words, but his actions. He never once said anything about showing up to watch me, but the fact that he came to silently support me makes my heart swoon.

Is this the Hayden no one else gets to see?

"You wouldn't have surprised me." I smile at him. "I mean, you did surprise me being here, but I'm glad you came."

He raises an eyebrow at me, a wave of shock passing through his eyes. "You are?"

"I am," I admit, swallowing hard over the lump that lodges itself in my throat. "That way you could see that figure skaters are just as skilled as hockey players."

"Shit," Hayden chuckles, the sound vibrating against my eardrums. "If I even tried to do some of the things you were doing, I would definitely end up on my ass."

Laughter freely flows from my lips, and he makes me feel so carefree in the moment. It's easy to be around him, as much as I hate admitting it. Something about Hayden just instantly soothes my soul. We walk side by side to our cars, Hayden walking over to my door with me.

Turning around to face him, he's standing closer

than I expected. I have to tilt my head back to look up at him, given our height difference. "So, you admit that figure skaters are better than hockey players?"

The smile plays on his lips as he steps closer into my space. He shakes his head as his fingertips brush against my face, sending a shiver down my spine as he tucks a stray hair behind my ear.

"Seeing you tonight..." he pauses, a wave of emotion passing through his eyes as he stares into my soul. "I've never witnessed something so beautiful. You were completely in your element, Eden," he breathes, sliding his palm along the side of my face. "You belong on the ice, creating art like you did tonight. Words really don't come close to touching how amazing that was to experience."

My breath catches in my throat as I get lost in his eyes. Our surroundings fade and nothing else matters in this moment, except the way he's staring at me. There's nothing but honesty in his words. His gaze is penetrating and I feel him carving his way through my rib cage and into my heart.

"I'm really happy you came," I breathe, reveling in the warmth of his palm cupping the side of my face. "I didn't ask you to come because I was afraid to."

Hayden's eyes bounce back and forth between mine, his eyebrows pulling together slightly. "Why would you be afraid to ask me?"

I shrug, attempting to brush away the awkwardness of my admission. I'm not usually this transparent with him—or anyone for that matter—but I can't help it when the honest words just flow from me without any care of the consequences.

"We agreed this was like a weird benefits thing... or whatever the hell it is." I pause, attempting to choose my words carefully because I'm not sure how to navigate this. I've never been in this situation with someone before. "I don't know. You know, we're not really friends—we're not really anything. It just seemed more like a friend move or strings attached if I were to invite you."

Hayden's face falls for a moment and he's silent as he stares back at me. I swallow roughly over the emotion in my throat. I hate this; I hate him for all of this. He was my enemy before, but now I'm quite positive I might hate him more than I did before.

And that's simply because I'm realizing that I don't actually hate him at all.

These feelings, I need to shut them off. They're only going to get me hurt, but I don't know how to do it. Hayden and I aren't the same. He might be able to disconnect, and I thought I could—fuck, I really didn't think it would be a problem. But now, I'm beginning to wonder if I may have made the biggest mistake of my life by getting involved with him like this.

"Eden," Hayden breathes, his voice strained and thick with emotion as his eyes search mine. He lifts his other hand, cupping both sides of my face as his gaze burns into mine. "Don't ever be afraid to ask me. Of course, I would want to come and support you. Look, I don't know what this is either. I told you we're going with it and even if we aren't friends, like you claim, that doesn't mean there are strings attached. You're a part of my life, regardless of how you may be in it. You matter to me, and I want you to share these parts of your life with me."

His words completely throw me off-balance. I feel unsteady on my feet, my knees weak as my heart pounds erratically inside my chest. How can he say such sweet, meaningful things when all we really are is fuck buddies?

"Why would you want me to share any parts of my life with you?"

Hayden's throat bobs as he swallows, his tongue slipping out as he wets his lips. They part slightly, as if the words linger just on the tip, but instead he lets out a ragged breath. A wave of torment passes through his eyes, almost as if he's at war with himself, before his lips crash into mine.

He steals the air from my lungs as his mouth moves against mine. My head swims and I'm lost to the moment, completely lost in him. Sliding my hands up the front of his body, I grab fistfuls of his winter coat. His hands are in my hair, his tongue sliding into my mouth, and my head is soaring in the clouds.

Fisting his coat in my hands, I hold on to him for dear life. He's the anchor holding me above water right now. I'm afraid to let go, afraid that none of this is real. And more importantly, I'm terrified to get lost in his stormy waters.

Because I know that once I'm lost in them, I will never come back up for air.

I'd drown in Hayden King, letting him drag me to the bottom of his ocean.

CHAPTER TWENTY

HAYDEN

As I sit on the bench, dressed in my gear for the game, I can't help but let my mind wander to Eden. Last night was unexpected. Well, not entirely. I had planned the whole thing, as far as waiting for her outside after the competition was over. But our conversation wasn't something I had expected.

I had been trying so hard to keep things at face value with her. Feelings aren't something that can exist between the two of us. Every time I'm around her, I find a crack in the facade that is beginning to vanish altogether. It's hard to keep my guard up around her and keep her at arm's length —metaphorically.

Eden Finley is under my skin, she's in my soul and she's making herself a home inside my heart.

"Yo, you coming?" Logan's voice calls out as he pulls me out of my thoughts. Lifting my head, I notice the locker room is completely empty, except for him standing in the doorway. He holds his helmet in one hand and his stick in the other.

"Shit," I mumble, rising to my feet as I pull my helmet on and grab my gloves and stick. Logan waits for me by the door and doesn't step out into the hall without me. We both head down the tunnel that leads to the rink.

Logan pauses as we reach the door, turning to face me. "What's going on with you, King?" he questions me with a worried tone, a look of concern in his eyes. "You've been off lately and I'm worried about you."

"It's nothing," I tell him dismissively, attempting to shrug it off. "I've just had a lot on my mind."

"It doesn't have anything to do with Eden Finley, does it?"

A sigh slips from my lips and I inhale deeply as I hang my head in defeat. Logan is silent, even though we both needed to be on the ice a few minutes ago. He doesn't leave, staying by my side like he always has.

Lifting my head, my gaze meets his. "I don't know what the fuck to do, bro."

"Things starting to get complicated?" he asks, a smirk tugging on the corner of his lips.

"You have no fucking clue," I mutter, shaking my head at him.

Logan puts his hand on my shoulder. "Trust me, Hayden. I know exactly how it goes and how it fucks with your head. Just be real with her, and don't be afraid to let her in."

"What good is that going to do? You know how I roll, Logan. I don't get involved with girls like that. I don't do relationships, because there's no way I can make a commitment like that."

"No one is telling you to sign your life over to her, Hayden," he scoffs, rolling his eyes as he pushes me toward the ice. We both file out and begin to skate over to the bench where the guys are all sitting. "Just go with it and see what happens. You'd be surprised what might happen if you let her see the side that everyone close to you gets. Believe it or not, she might actually like you then."

"Fuck you, Knight," I laugh, attempting to hit him with my stick, but he ducks out of the way, hopping over the boards and onto the bench. I follow after him and we both get glares from the other guys. Coach notices us and scowls.

"Did the two of you forget that we have a game to play tonight?"

Logan and I both look up at him, but of course it's me and my dumb ass who has to say something. "Not at all." I instantly regret it, by the way he narrows his eyes at us. He doesn't appreciate people not being punctual. Especially when it comes to our games. He sees it as us not taking it seriously.

"The two of you better play your asses off tonight or you can plan on not getting any game time next week."

I open my mouth up to say something that I shouldn't, but Logan notices it quick enough. He drives his elbow into my side and even though I can't feel it through my pads, it's enough to make me shut my mouth and nod.

Logan and I are the two best defensemen on our team, so we're always on the ice together and usually we're out first. Everyone lines up and I see August's name and the number 19 on the back of his jersey as he leans down for the face-off.

My heart pounds rapidly in my chest, the adrenaline steadily coursing through my veins as it feels like time is suspended in air. The ref finally drops the puck and I watch as August battles with his opponent until he effectively wins the face-off, sending the puck toward Simon.

He passes it back to Logan, who skates around as one of the offensive players comes toward him. His stick slides across the ice as he effortlessly passes it past the left winger. August is right there to receive it and has a breakaway as he begins to skate toward the net. Logan and I hang back, slowly skating as we stay in our zone, and watch our guys make moves.

This is how the game usually goes, until the puck ends up back in our zone and it's time for us to defend the goal. Asher is an exceptional goalie, but we're always the front line, making sure no one fucks with him and that the puck stays out of our net.

We play back and forth, our team taking it down the ice, attempting a few shots at the goal, before it's repeated on our side. This team is definitely more skilled than the one we played last week. It's time for shift change and Logan and I skate back to the bench as Greyson and Vaughn begin to skate back to the center of the ice.

Leaning forward, I prop my elbows on my knees and watch as they line up for another face-off. The ref skates toward the middle of them, holding the puck in the air as they line up their sticks, their bodies bent forward slightly. The ref drops the puck and they fight over it until it's won again by our team.

At least our team has a higher percentage of winning them.

I feel like since Eden entered my life, I've been in more face-offs than I ever have been before.

And I haven't won a single one.

———

Everyone is exhausted after the game and thankfully, there are no plans made to go out. I don't think I have it in me to go pretend to be enjoying my time getting drunk with them. It sounds really fucked up, because that's what I've been doing for quite some time now, but it just isn't as fulfilling.

As much as I love the guys—they're practically family—I'm tired of the same old shit. I need something new and I've found the perfect person to occupy my time with.

And now that's the only thing I want to do if I'm not busy with hockey.

Skipping the showers in the locker room, I drive home drenched in sweat with that lovely hockey smell no one enjoys. It's actually a pretty gross smell. Like sweat and corn chips had a baby. Don't question me on it, but I swear that's what it smells like. Maybe with something musty thrown in there too.

Either way, I stink and head home to get a shower instead. Simon and Sterling both went out to get beers and food. I plan on heating up something that is left over in the fridge and passing out on the couch while watching *SportsCenter*. All of the guys who are wifed up don't go out much anymore, and I'm beginning to understand why.

After showering, I find some leftover pasta in the fridge and throw it into the microwave before settling on the couch. It's nice and quiet in the house, although it's lonely. And not from the guys not being here... there's something else missing.

Eden.

Reaching into the front pocket of my hoodie, I pull out my phone and unlock the screen. Last night after seeing Eden, I made sure to get her phone number. She didn't hesitate to give it to me and I'm not hesitating to use it at this moment. Opening up my messages, I click on the icon to start a new message and select Eden's name.

HAYDEN

Hey you. If you're sleeping, I hope I
didn't wake you up.

I get half the urge to erase the entire thing and
send something that doesn't sound like I'm being
too forward. How the hell do I tell her I was thinking
about her without sounding like I'm obsessed...
which isn't necessarily a stretch anymore.

Turning my attention back to the TV, I lock my
phone and set it on the couch beside me. It can't be
more than a minute before I notice it vibrating next
to me as a new message comes through. I can't fight
the grin on my face as I pick it back up and quickly
tap on it.

EDEN

You didn't wake me. How was your
game tonight?

The grin is still on my face, my heart crawling
into my throat. I didn't tell her I had a game,
although I'm sure she knows the game schedule
with being at the rink all the time. None of that
matters, though. The fact that she cared enough to
take an interest is more than enough for me.

HAYDEN

We won. It wasn't an easy one, but we managed. How was your night?

I see the bubbles pop up as she begins to type a response. Holding on to my phone, I set my plate of food down and ignore that and the TV as I wait for Eden to say something.

EDEN

Oh, it was exhilarating. I caught up on some schoolwork and have just been laying in bed watching TV.

The image of her in bed has my cock waking up. I've seen how Eden looks in her bed and in my own, and that is a memory I'll never be able to get out of my head.

HAYDEN

What are you wearing, baby?

Things have been getting complicated between the two of us and right now, I'm fucking horny and need to chase away the feelings she ignites inside me. It's easier and lighter if I switch it over to something to distract both of us.

And Eden Finley just so happens to be my favorite distraction.

EDEN

A tank top and boy shorts.

She doesn't miss a beat and I fucking love it. My cock grows in my pants, thinking of her with barely anything on. I know what's underneath those clothes and I want to feel her beneath me right now.

HAYDEN

Send me a pic.

EDEN

In your dreams, King.

She's feisty and her attitude has me wrapping my free hand around my cock.

HAYDEN

I know where you live, Finley. Don't make me come over uninvited.

EDEN

You wouldn't dare...

HAYDEN

Is that a challenge? Don't underestimate me, baby.

My grip tightens around my cock as I continue to stroke it. I'm still home alone, but I'm about to leave and go fuck this girl into oblivion.

EDEN

What if that's what I want?

HAYDEN

Then you get what you want.

She doesn't respond right away and I check my phone again, watching the bubbles appear and then disappear. Finally they pop back up and stay until she sends another message.

EDEN

As much as I'd love for you to show up, Winter's had her sister staying with us since the showcase last night. They just got back from dinner and I promised them I would watch a movie with them.

A groan falls from my lips and I tilt my head back for a moment before looking back at my phone.

HAYDEN

Fuck them. Come over here.

EDEN

Sorry, babe, not tonight. One night this week, though?

As much as I want to argue with her, as badly as I want to go show up at her apartment and drag her

out to my car, I know I can't. There has to be bound-
aries, and I have to respect them. Even if it means
she's leaving me with my hand and my memories of
her tonight.

HAYDEN

I don't have practice on
Wednesday. Come over then.

EDEN

I'll be there. And we can finish what
we started tonight...

Goddamn, she really knows how to fuck with my
head. I don't know what we're doing anymore, but
we're sure as fuck playing with fire.

And we're bound to get burned.

CHAPTER TWENTY-ONE
EDEN

Pulling up to Hayden's house, my stomach is in my throat from my anxiety. It's certainly not the first time we've hung out, but usually it's later at night. It's only a little after dinnertime, so it feels kind of weird coming to hang out with him. We had an agreement of keeping things at face value so I'm trying to do what he said and not overthink.

But I can't help but feel like this is something more than it actually is.

We aren't friends. We aren't anything. We don't hang out and do friend activities like this. We just meet up when one of us has an itch to scratch and fall in bed together. After that, we go our separate ways like we've never connected. Me back to hating him and Hayden back to doing whatever the hell it is that he does.

After he showed up at my last skating showcase, things just feel... different. I don't know how to explain it, mainly because I don't want to put more thought into it than I have. If I overthink it into something it isn't, it will absolutely crush me when the truth comes out.

I find a parking spot on the street and pull out my phone as I get out of my car. Finding the message thread with Hayden, I send him a text, letting him know I'm here. Expecting a response from him, I slow my footsteps as I get closer to the front door. He still hasn't said anything and I'm beginning to wonder if this was a bad idea.

I should have checked in with him before tonight about hanging out, but whenever I spoke to him, our conversations never allowed for me to ask. And I didn't really think he would bail or stand me up. If he didn't want to hang out, I would have thought he would have texted me and said so. And since he seems to enjoy texting me daily, it should have come up.

As I reach the bottom step that leads up to his front porch, I pause for a moment, contemplating my next move. Glancing down at my phone, I see Hayden still hasn't responded. I could just text him now and go back home, where I know I'm safe and don't have to face possible disappointment.

Looking up at the house, I notice most of the lights are on and it seems like there's someone moving around inside. It could simply be Simon and Sterling, and Hayden might not even be here.

Inhaling deeply, I push my shoulders back and gather all of the confidence I can muster. Disappointment is everywhere, regardless of where we go and what we do. If I leave now, it's still there, regardless of me walking up to the front door or not. Hayden and I had plans, so that's what I'm here for. I'll worry about the rest, depending on how this goes.

I walk up the front steps, my gait light as I walk across the wooden porch before stopping in front of the door. My finger finds the doorbell and I press down on it, taking a step back as I wrap my coat tighter around my body to shield myself from the cold gusts of air. No one comes at first and I shift my weight, feeling dread rolling in the pit of my stomach.

This is exactly what I feared would happen. If I would have just walked away and got in my car, I wouldn't be slapped in the face with this moment. The moment where I look like a fool, standing outside his house and he's nowhere to be seen.

A defeated sigh slips from my lips and I tuck my chin to my chest, before I turn around and begin to walk down the steps. As I'm halfway down to the sidewalk, I hear the door behind me open in a rush.

"Eden," Hayden breathes, and I can hear the confusion in his voice. "Where are you going?"

Turning around, I lift my chin to look at him. "Home," I shrug dismissively, "I didn't think you were here."

"I am," he says, stepping out into the coldness of the evening with just a pair of sweatpants on. My throat constricts, my eyes dropping to his bare chest for a moment as I trace the planes of his body that my hands have touched many times before. He's perfectly chiseled, not too muscular but thin with definition. "I'm sorry. I was getting a quick shower and I told the guys to answer the door if you came, but they must not have heard the doorbell ring."

My gaze travels up to his wet hair, hanging in a tousled mess just above his eyebrows. My heart is in my throat with the way he's looking at me, a desperate, pleading look passing through his stormy eyes.

Inhaling deeply, I begin to ascend back up the steps, only stopping as I reach him on the front porch.

Relief floods his expression and the corners of his lips twitch. "Stay?"

This is the Hayden King I was afraid of getting close to. The one who can melt the ice around my heart with the sound of his voice and the look in his eyes.

We're silent for a moment, lost in each other's burning gaze as his question hangs in the air around us. I don't need to answer it, though, because we both already know I'm not going anywhere.

"Are you going to invite me in or are we going to stand out here until we turn into ice sculptures?"

Hayden chuckles, stepping out of the way as he waves me in. "You already are one, baby. The most ethereal, angelic one I've ever laid my eyes on."

I can't stop the laughter that falls from my lips as I attempt to ignore the fluttering in my stomach. Walking past him, I step inside as he follows behind and pulls the door shut, locking out the cold air.

"You know, you don't have to do that," I tell him, looking at him over my shoulder as I shrug off my coat.

Hayden takes it from me and hangs it up in the foyer as he raises an eyebrow. "Do what?"

"Say things like that to me," I shrug, attempting to make the conversation more casual than the emotional undertone that lingers. "I'm already here. You don't have to whisper sweet nothings to make me feel good or to try and get me in bed. I don't need that from you."

Hayden's face contorts slightly, his eyebrows pulling together as a wave of something indistinguishable passes through his features. I half expect him to argue, but instead he just nods, falling silent before walking past me. There's a weird shift and I feel uncomfortable as I follow him into the house.

He walks into the living room and I'm surprised when I see no one else is in there. The massive TV that is positioned on the wall has a list of movies up. Hayden walks over to the couch and drops down before glancing over at me as I awkwardly stand in the center of the room.

"Come sit with me," he says softly, a smile forming on his lips as he places his arm on the back of the couch. "I don't bite... unless you're into that."

A laugh gets caught in my throat and a strangled choking sound comes out instead. I feel the heat creeping up my neck before it spreads across my cheeks. Ducking my head, I shuffle my feet across the rug and drop down onto the couch next to him.

Hayden wraps his arm around the tops of my shoulders and I relax against him, reveling in his familiarity and comfortableness. Any awkward feelings I was having instantly vanish as soon as I'm cocooned in his warm arms.

"I thought maybe we could do something different tonight and watch a movie," he murmurs, gently pressing his lips against the top of my head. My eyelids fall shut for a moment and I inhale deeply, attempting to calm my heart as it threatens to break free from its cage.

"That sounds nice," I whisper, not fully trusting my voice. This is completely different for us, but it's scary how normal it feels. Hayden picks up the remote and begins to go through the list of different movies.

I lean my head against his chest, not even paying attention to what he's doing on the TV. With my ear pressed against him, I listen to the soft thumping of his heart and his voice as it vibrates inside his rib cage.

"You want to watch a horror movie?" he questions me as he lazily traces his fingers over my bare arm.

"Sure," I agree, glancing at the TV even though I couldn't care less what is on there. "You pick."

Hayden settles on the newest Halloween movie, which is one I haven't seen yet. The whole horror movie charade is completely overplayed, but I'll play along with him. He already has me in his arms, so I'm not sure what more he could want by trying to scare me with a movie. What he doesn't know about me is that I'm quite the horror buff. So, it's laughable that I'm in this position right now.

Turning to face the TV, I position my back against his side and Hayden lazily drapes his arms around me. We both fall into a silence as we watch the TV and the movie begins. Just as it starts the opening scene, Hayden grabs the remote and pauses it.

"Do you want popcorn or a drink or something?" he questions me with a nervousness in his voice. I can't help but smile as he searches my eyes with a panicked look.

Dear God, Hayden has really never done this before.

Bless his little playboy heart.

"Sure," I smile at him. "Can I use your bathroom quick?" I don't really have to go, but in this moment, I don't know what else to do. Sit here and stare at the paused TV screen or follow him into the kitchen like a lost puppy?

Hayden nods as he rises to his feet. "If you go upstairs, it's the first door on your right."

I watch as he quickly disappears from the living room and slips into the kitchen. My footsteps are light on the floor as I make my way back to the foyer of the house and practically skip up the stairs. As I reach the second floor, it looks exactly like I would expect it to look with a group of guys living here.

The downstairs was much cleaner than I had expected, but up here is a different story. There's random hockey equipment throughout the hall and scattered clothes. Whoever cleaned downstairs needs to come up here and do the same. I notice a few closed doors, two of them with the light peeking underneath.

Just as I reach the bathroom, one of the doors opens and Sterling steps out. His eyes meet mine, widening slightly as he pauses in the middle of the hall.

"Hey, Eden," he says slowly, as if he's approaching a spooked animal. The way he's acting makes my heart constrict. There was a point where Sterling and I were close. We had a lot of classes together and he was new on the hockey team his freshman year, while Chance was a senior. Chance took him under his wing to show him the ropes and in the process, we became really good friends.

Sterling was Chance's best friend, at least for that last year he was around. I couldn't stay friends with Sterling after the breakup. It was just too painful for me, and he was too close to it all. I didn't know the status of their friendship after Chance went to play professionally and, to be honest, I didn't care to know anything about it.

"Hey, Sterling," I offer in a friendly tone as I hover by the bathroom door. Suddenly I wish I would have decided to stay downstairs as I stare back at my old friend. "How are you?"

He completely ignores my question, his lips turning downward. "You and Hayden are hanging out, right? He told us he had someone coming over, but didn't say who. I figured it was you."

I cut my eyes at him. "Why does it matter what I'm doing?"

"Just be careful with him," he warns, his throat bobbing as he swallows. "I saw how things ended with you and Orion and I would hate to see it go the same way with King."

"I can take care of myself, but thanks, Sterling," I quip, rolling my eyes at him. "I know exactly what

I'm getting into with Hayden, and that's between the two of us, not you."

"Yeah, I know," he says, his voice filled with defeat as he hangs his head for a moment. "I just don't want to see you get hurt again. We were close at one point, Eden. I still care about you as a friend, like I did back then."

A harsh laugh falls from my lips and I have no intention of stopping it as I glare at Sterling. "Is that so? I can tell that you really cared about me back then. You were so far up Chance's ass, you of all people should have known his intentions, and you didn't even think to give me a heads-up about it."

"Are you kidding me?" he throws back at me, crossing his arms over his chest. "He played us all, Eden. You aren't the only one he left behind."

I stare at him for a moment, my body falling rigid as guilt rushes through my body. "What do you mean?"

"When he left, he wrote us all off. No one heard from him again after he started playing for the NHL. We were all just stepping stones to Orion, none of us actually mattered."

I never once considered it as a possibility. I was too caught up in my own heartbreak from Chance Orion, that I never thought about him leaving everyone else. Severing all of the ties he had from his old life. There was a part of me that was convinced he and Sterling would have stayed friends, but hearing him now, it all makes sense.

"I'm really sorry, Sterling," I tell him, my voice soft and quiet. I can't help but feel terrible for him in this moment as the truth finally surfaces. "I had no idea."

"How could you possibly have known?" he questions me, his voice harsh as he uncrosses his arms and shoves his hands in the front pocket of his hoodie. "You were too wrapped up in yourself and what you were going through to even pay attention to anyone else."

His words are like a slap across the face, the sting lingering as I stare back at him. Sterling's chest rises as he inhales deeply. I watch the torment on his face as he shakes his head at me.

"None of it matters now, Eden," he says in resignation, exhaling deeply. "I just hope you know what you're doing with King."

"I do," I tell him, swallowing hard over the lump lodged in my throat.

"Good," he nods as he turns around to head back to his bedroom, "because when he gets drafted, don't be surprised if he pulls the same kind of shit."

Sterling leaves me in the hallway with his words hanging heavily in the air. I hate to think about them, but he's completely right. Nothing good will ever come from this with Hayden. He'll leave me in the end, when it's his time to move on in life.

And I just signed myself up for another heartbreak.

CHAPTER TWENTY-TWO
HAYDEN

It's been a few days of the same thing with Eden. I've been trying to get closer to her but there has been a shift in the wrong direction. Instead of her ice melting, it's almost as if she's had a guard up even more. When I'm around her, she's still herself with me, but a little more reserved.

I noticed the night I invited her over to watch a movie. She was silent for most of it, which was fine. I had her come over with good intentions, not to try and get her in my bed and have it be that. I know keeping it that way was the original plan, but plans constantly change.

I want more from her than just her body. I want her mind, her soul, every fucking piece she will give me.

But the more I try to get inside, the more she seems to block me out. She hasn't been avoiding me like she did in the beginning. I see her more often than I ever have in the past year we've been attending the same university.

Most nights, she either ends up here or I end up at her place. She doesn't like to talk much and whenever I try to open the door for conversation, she shuts me down. I don't know what happened, but it's really fucking strange.

As I sit at the kitchen island, I replay that night over in my head, thinking of what could have set her off. She was fine until she went to the bathroom, and then she came back different. Did she get a phone call or a text? I didn't hear her phone go off at all throughout the rest of the evening.

She went upstairs to the bathroom... and Sterling and Simon were both up there.

Just as the thought enters my mind, Sterling comes strolling into the kitchen to make his typical morning protein shake. Lifting my head, my gaze meets his and I narrow my eyes at him.

"Did you see Eden when she was here last week?"

Sterling shrugs. "I don't remember. She's been here a lot, so I'm sure I did."

My eyes slice to his. "Don't bullshit me, Sterling. What did you say to her?"

He rolls his eyes, an exasperated sigh escaping him as he turns his back to me and pulls open the fridge. "I told her the truth. That I don't want to see her get hurt again like she did with Orion."

What the fuck.

"Why the hell would you say anything to her?" I can't help the anger that is boiling inside of me in this moment. I knew there had to have been something that caused the shift in the way Eden was acting toward me. And this entire time, it's been right in front of my face. My own fucking friend who is supposed to have my back.

"Because you didn't see how she fell apart when things ended between them, Hayden," he says, as he puts his hands on the counter and leans on them. His eyes stare into mine, not with any anger or animosity, but instead they're filled with concern. "She took it fucking hard. It bothered me that she wrote off our friendship, but it hurt even more to see how broken she was because of him."

"I'm not going to do that to her, Sterling," I tell him, my voice desperate with my plea. "I know I don't have the best track record with girls and lord knows I have no idea what to do when it comes to relationships. But hurting Eden is nowhere on my to-do list in life."

Sterling tilts his head to the side, curiosity in his gaze. "So, what happens after graduation? Say you get drafted and have to move across the country. Then what happens with you and Eden?"

I stare at him for a moment, considering his words. There's nothing malicious behind what he's saying. Instead, he's trying to get me to look at the whole picture. To look into the future—somewhere further than I normally look. And I haven't even considered what would happen then.

"I don't know," I tell him honestly. "I haven't thought that far ahead. Nothing between us is even definitive. We both decided to take it for whatever it was and just have fun with it. I don't know what the fuck happens next, Sterling."

"Well, that's something you need to consider," he says matter-of-factly as he pushes off the counter. I watch him as he collects all of the ingredients for his shake and throws them into the blender. "Eden Finley isn't a temporary kind of girl. She might have you fooled right now, but she doesn't just take things for whatever they might be. If you guys have an agreement, then I hope to God you're actually on the same page and not the one she's showing you."

"What's that supposed to mean?"

Sterling sighs. "Eden plays everything close to her chest. She's not going to reveal all of her cards if she doesn't know what you're holding. I know her well enough to know there is more to her than the two of you are making it out to be."

"So, what am I supposed to do?" I'm at a loss. I don't know the first thing about being in a relationship with someone and I don't know if that's what I want with Eden. All I know is, I don't want her to have that with anyone else. I want her to myself.

Sterling stares at me for a moment. "Don't fuck it up."

———

After finding out the ice schedule, I now know that Eden has been using the open ice time at the beginning of the day. She's in and out before most of us are even out of bed. Not this morning, though. She didn't see me when I arrived at the rink a few minutes after her.

And she didn't even notice me as I hovered in the stands while she effortlessly floated around the rink.

She skated for a solid hour and a half before exiting through the tunnel. After exiting the stands, I made my way downstairs to where the locker rooms are. As I turn the corner and head toward the rooms, I see her as she slips out, dressed with her coat and winter boots on.

Eden swings her bag over her shoulder, her head lifting as her gaze meets mine. A smirk forms on my lips as her eyes widen and she halts mid-step. "What are you doing here?"

I walk up to her, stopping once I reach her. "I could ask you the same thing."

"Are you stalking me now?"

Laughter vibrates in my chest and I watch her face scrunch up in irritation. "Maybe I am. Maybe I'm not. You tell me, Finley. Do you want me to be your stalker?"

"Don't be a creep, King," she laughs, shaking her head. "But seriously, what are you doing here? I thought you didn't have practice until tonight."

"I don't," I tell her, shrugging. "I knew you would be here and I wanted to see you."

Her lips part slightly, her face relaxing as she shifts her weight on her feet. It's obvious the effect I have on her, and I let it fuel my ego. It's probably a little unhealthy, but she's not stupid. Eden knows the power she holds over me as well.

"I mean, you do have my number... you could have called or texted me instead."

"What would be the fun in that?" I ask her, tilting my head to the side as I raise an eyebrow. "Plus, I like watching you skate and you're never here when I am."

She's silent again, almost as if she doesn't know how to respond. I take that as my cue to keep talking. She has a way of making me question everything and if I don't ask her now, I don't know that I ever will.

"I have an away game this weekend and I want you to come with me."

Eden raises an eyebrow at me. "You want me to go away with you for the weekend?"

I nod, holding back the laugh at her literally repeating what I just said. "Yeah. I have to ride to and from the game with the team and stay with them. But I was thinking, if you came and got a hotel room, I could sneak out and see you."

"Couldn't that get you in a lot of trouble?"

A smirk plays on my lips. "Only if I get caught."

The lilt of Eden's laughter is like music to my soul.

The sound slides over my eardrums like silk and I want to live in this moment. The sound of her—just being in her presence—is intoxicating. "You really want me to?"

"More than anything."

Eden's silent for a moment before the corners of her lips lift. "Then I'll follow you for the weekend."

Letting out the breath I didn't realize I was holding, relief washes over me. I can't help but want her to take that sentence back and change the wording. I don't just want her to follow me for the weekend. I want her to follow me through life.

Although, that's not an option. Eden and I both live two separate lives. One of us is going to have to make a sacrifice at some point. We have separate dreams, ones that don't exactly coincide. I don't know how to make it work, but I'm at the point where I would consider following her instead of expecting her to follow me.

Whether it's our hearts or our skates... one will suffer in the end.

CHAPTER TWENTY-THREE
EDEN

"You getting ready to leave?" Winter asks me as she pokes her head in through the door to my bedroom. I'm sitting on the floor, putting things into my suitcase, as she steps inside. I lift my gaze to hers, watching her as she drops down onto the floor beside me.

"Yeah. Hayden said they would be leaving around ten so I thought I would leave around the same time."

Winter stares at me for a moment. "Did you get your hotel figured out?"

I nod. "It's only two blocks away from the arena they're playing at."

Hayden was the one who found the hotel and booked the room for me. I had called and tried to get the payment changed, because the last thing I wanted was for him to be paying for stuff for me. They wouldn't let me change it without contacting him, so I let it go. Hayden was pissed when I told him about it, but whatever.

We're not anything. I have to keep reminding myself of that fact when he continues to do nice things for me like I'm actually his girlfriend.

"What's really going on with the two of you?" Winter questions me as she picks up a pair of jeans and folds them for me. "I haven't wanted to pry, but the two of you have been spending a lot of time together... and now you're going away with him for the weekend."

"Well, not really. I'm just going to watch him play and spend the night there."

Winter purses her lips, giving me a knowing look that is laced with disapproval. "Come on, Eden. Admit it. You're in deep with Hayden King, and you fucking love it."

My breath catches in my throat. Swallowing roughly over the knives that cut through my flesh, I shake my head, refusing to speak it into the universe. "We're just messing around, Winter. It's seriously nothing. It's a nice distraction from the monotony of life and it's fun."

Winter shakes her head. "No. You don't get to put your frigid walls up with me, Eden. I can see through your bullshit and I see how you are with him. It may have started off that way, but the two of you are both in so far over your heads, neither of you know which way is up or down."

Emotion builds inside me and I busy myself with my hands, shoving things into my suitcase. I hate this feeling, the uncertainty of it all. I don't know Hayden's feelings, so that makes it harder for me to admit mine. I can't let myself get lost in him when he has made it clear he doesn't do relationships. At this point, I'm literally asking for him to break my heart.

"You're in love with him, aren't you?"

Fuck.

"No," I shake my head and clear my throat as I zip my suitcase shut, "I don't even like him, Winter."

"You're a terrible liar."

Rising to my feet, I lift my bag and set it on my bed. "I know," I whisper, not fully trusting my voice. "I never should have gotten involved with him."

Winter chuckles. "It's a little late for that now," she offers as she stands up and turns to look at me. "What happens now? Are you going to tell him how you feel?"

I snort. "What good would that do anyone?"

"I've seen the way he looks at you and how he acts around you. You might be surprised to find that he feels the same way you do."

The thought alone is quite comical. I can't help it as a harsh laugh escapes me. "That is laughable."

"When the two of you are alone this weekend, if it feels right, tell him," Winter urges before she walks back through the doorway. She pauses in the hall, turning to face me one last time. "Life is too short, Eden. You don't want to look back and have regrets one day. Don't let him be the one who got away."

Winter leaves me with her words hanging heavily in the air. My heart pounds rapidly in my chest at the thought alone—the possibility of sharing my feelings with Hayden and him feeling the same way. I understand what she's saying, about life being too short. But is it short enough that it's worth the heartbreak or the disappointment?

It's almost as if I've gotten too comfortable with Hayden and the way things are between us. Thinking about messing that up gives me serious anxiety. And if I share my feelings with him, it's bound to change everything between us. I can't be the one who makes the first move where feelings are concerned. I'll leave that ball in Hayden's court.

And if he doesn't share anything with me before graduation, then I suppose what's meant to be will be.

———

The drive to the hotel wasn't as long as it seemed. It took a few hours, but sometimes longer car rides can be relaxing. Having the ability to complete a mindless task like driving and having a long concert with yourself. Playing your music loud and singing your little heart out when there's no one around to hear how terrible you sing.

Hayden texted me a few times while I was driving, and I tried to respond until he told me not to because he didn't want me to not focus on the road. I hate when he does things like that. I wish he would just pretend that he doesn't care. If he didn't care, it would make this a lot simpler. That was what we agreed to—the simplicity of this arrangement. Not the complications that are quickly arising.

I check into my room and send Hayden a text when I get onto the elevator, letting him know everything is going well. He responds, letting me know they're already on campus and in the guest dorms they're staying in for the night. As I reach the twenty-second floor and find my hotel room, Hayden tells me they're heading to the rink soon and for me to be there around six-thirty, since the game starts at seven.

As I walk into the hotel room, I swear I'm taken completely by surprise. It's massive, especially for one person and one night. It's a goddamn suite instead of a typical hotel room. Leaving my suitcase in the middle of the room, I walk over to the wall that is entirely made of windows and look out. It looks over the entire city and it's absolutely breathtaking.

I'm not one for heights, but being able to see out across the horizon, there's something that makes it seem majestic. Not only the buildings and the city buzzing beneath, but you can see the mountains in the horizon. Each cap is dusted with snow. It's like something out of a painting and I'm lost for a moment, staring at the world's beauty.

Finally pulling myself away from the windows, I walk back through the hotel room and take my bag into the bedroom. I pause in the doorway, my heart crawling into my throat as my eyes fall on the massive king-sized bed across from me. There are deep red rose petals scattered on top of the comforter, falling onto the floor as they leave a trail.

The petals are arranged in the shape of a heart and I notice a folded jersey in the center. As I reach for it, I see a handwritten note, no doubt from Hayden, tucked in the collar of it. Taking the jersey, I hold it up, noticing the Wyncote Wolves on the front. As I turn it around, I see King written in bold white letters across the top with the number 8 underneath.

Wear this for me for good luck tonight, baby. I'd love to see you wearing my number.

Love, Hayden

My heart is in my throat as I clutch the jersey close to my chest and hold the note in one hand. Noticing the trail of petals on the floor, my feet take over and I follow them over to the Jacuzzi tub, where there are various salt scrubs and candles around it. None of them are lit, thankfully. I don't know who Hayden paid to do all of this, but there's no way I'm letting him get away with it.

My heart melts, the ice pooling around my feet as it turns to liquid. I'm so torn between it all. Part of me wants to slap him and tell him to knock it off. That we don't do this kind of stuff. We're not in a relationship, we're not even friends. He can't do this —my heart literally can't handle it.

And the other part of me wants to swoon. To say fuck it all and lose myself in him completely.

I'm at war with myself, and it takes everything in me to turn around and get back to what I really need to do here. Lifting my suitcase onto the bed, I pull out my outfit for the game tonight and carry it into the bathroom with me. After stripping out of my clothes, I step into the hot water of the shower to wash my body.

I've never been to any of Hayden's games before, so this is a first for me. We never talked about me coming to any of his home games and even though they're open to the public, I couldn't bring myself to show up. I wanted him to invite me. And here I am now... in a completely different city to watch him play this weekend.

This is one thing that Chance never did. He never asked me to go away with him and watch him play. He barely even invited me to his home games, but I still showed up because that's what you do when you're committed to someone. You support them endlessly and follow them to the ends of the earth to witness their dreams come true.

There was a time where I would have done that for Chance. With the way my life has worked out, I'm glad I didn't. I'm glad he ended things because while I was with him, I forgot about myself. And that is one thing I will never let happen again.

Regardless of what happens with Hayden and me, I refuse to give up my own dreams.

I won't put myself second to someone else again.

CHAPTER TWENTY-FOUR
HAYDEN

As we file into the locker room, it's like I'm thrown back in time, to a place I never want to visit again. It's my first time being in one of the away team's locker rooms, but it looks exactly like the home team's. This used to be my home team. And I'm so glad it's not anymore.

Last year, when I came to Wyncote, I was able to avoid playing the Panthers—the team I used to play for. They only matched up once or twice in a season and thankfully, those games were played before I moved. Now that I'm here, playing on the opposing side, it just feels fucking strange.

I fucked up when I was here. I never should have gotten involved with my coach's daughter. When we first hooked up, I didn't know who she was... until she showed up at one of our practices to talk to her dad. After that, I knew I needed to end shit with her. Not to mention the fact that she was pushing for more than I could give her.

Carly wanted a relationship and I didn't want anything with her. She didn't take it well and it became a huge fucking scandal. I hightailed it out of there and never looked back. But now I'm back and I don't fucking like it.

"Hey," Logan says as he walks over to me, a grim look on his face. "How are you doing? You look like you could puke."

"I mean, being here definitely has that effect," I tell him with a shrug as I pull my chest protector over my head. "No, I'm good, though. I just want to get this game over with and get the fuck out of here."

Logan nods, but doesn't offer any words. He doesn't need to because he understands. Logan, August, and Cam were all by my side when shit went down and went south. No words need to be spoken about it now because it's all in the past. There's nothing that can be done about it now. We just need to play this game so I can be done here.

Everyone is still getting dressed after I finish

tying my skates. Reaching into the front pocket of my bag, I pull out my phone to see if Eden said anything else to me. I look at the time and notice it's a little after six. I told her to be here around six-thirty, so I'm not sure if she's on her way or not.

HAYDEN

Hey you. Are you on your way to the rink yet?

EDEN

Just getting ready to leave now. Why aren't you on the ice?

A smile tugs at my lips. This girl doesn't miss a beat. Instead of feeding into the conversation, she's always quick to call me out and I love it. I love the challenge she presents.

HAYDEN

We're getting ready to go out in a few. I can't wait to see you.

EDEN

You better pay attention to the game and not to who is sitting in the stands.

This is the first time she's watching me play. I know she's seen me at practice before, but having her here at an actual game is something different. There isn't a need to impress her, but there's definitely some pressure to play my ass off. I don't want to look like a scrub on the ice with her watching me.

It's hard to not think about her sitting up there. I already know I'll be looking for her when I first get out there, but I'll have to push it from my mind and focus on the task at hand: beating the fucking Panthers so I can get back to my girl.

"You guys ready to go?" Asher calls from over by the doorway as his eyes scan the locker room. "Coach wants us out there to start practicing now."

Everyone practically jumps to their feet as the noise level rises and they all get hyped up. The energy in the room is fucking buzzing and like a high of its own. Looking down at my phone, I tap out another message to Eden.

HAYDEN

I gotta get on the ice, but I'll see you afterward. Wish me luck, baby.

I don't get the chance to wait for her response as August walks over and grabs my phone from me. Quickly rising to my feet, I narrow my eyes at him as I put my hand out. He laughs and completely bypasses my hand as he shoves it back into the pocket of my bag.

"Your girl will be waiting for you after the game," he says, clapping his hand on my shoulder as he attempts to usher me out of the room. "We need you to get your head in this shit and not worry about her right now."

Before giving me a chance to respond, August exits the locker room and I follow along behind him. He's right, and I need to follow his advice if I'm going to follow anyone's. Of all people, it has to be the hardest for August with a fiancée and a baby at home. It's not as easy for his girl, Poppy, to come watch with their little one that she's taking care of.

I have to give him all the credit in the world, though. I don't know how he does it. There's a part of me that thinks if I were in that situation, it would be impossible to leave them at home while I'm out playing. But then again, it's all in the name of the game. And if we all make it to a professional level, it's only going to get more intense, with more time away from our people.

We go through our warm-up on the ice, everyone working on their shots and stretching. Before I know it, the stands are beginning to fill up and it's almost time for the puck to drop. As we skate over to our lineup for the national anthem, I can't keep my eyes from looking around the arena. I don't see her at first, but when I do, it's almost as if everything around us vanishes.

Eden is behind our bench, about ten rows off the ice. She has a black beanie pulled over her head and she's wearing my jersey. I wasn't sure if she would or not, but I made sure there was one in her room waiting for her. A smile pulls on the corners of her lips as our gazes collide. She slowly raises her hand to me and I do the same, not giving a fuck if anyone notices.

We all line up for the face-off, with our normal line of guys out on the ice. I get into my defensive zone as Logan gets into his. The tension is high, adrenaline coursing through everyone's system as we stare at the ice, waiting to see the ref drop the puck. Suddenly, the black frozen disc hits the ice and the game is on.

August and the center from the other team battle over the puck. It doesn't take much for August to get it into our zone, passing it to one of our team-mates. Logan and I both hang back as we watch them skate toward the opposing goal. We move along the ice, following behind in case we need to intervene.

It isn't long into the first period before our team is already scoring a goal and it's time for me to let someone else on the ice. As I skate over to the bench, I lift my head, my eyes finding Eden in the crowd. She's smiling down at me, her eyes intense as she watches the entire game unfold.

It's a pretty mundane game. The Panthers have definitely gone to shit from when I played for them. By the time we get to the third period, we're beating them 5-1. And the only reason they managed to get a puck past Asher was because one of their teammates was fucking with him.

Believe it or not, the ref didn't call it, which is fairly typical for them. There's always dirty hits and shit that gets missed. Or sometimes it seems like they just don't even want to make the call. It's annoying as fuck, but that's where Logan and I come in as the enforcers. He tends to get into more fights than I do, but I'm never against it.

I know the guy who fucked with Asher. Number 87, Artemis. I played on the same goddamn team with him for two and a half seasons. He's as dirty as they come and he's a dumbass for thinking he could get one over on our goalie and get away with it.

Logan and I both hit the ice, Logan pointing over to Artemis across the rink. We both simultaneously nod and ignore the entire game as we power skate in his direction. Every now and then a lesson needs to be taught. Our team is a family and you don't fuck with our family.

And if someone chooses to, you go to war for them.

CHAPTER TWENTY-FIVE
EDEN

Sitting in the stands, I watch in awe as Hayden skates around the ice. He looks like he's at home, like he found the place where he belongs. The way he works with his team is incredible. Being a figure skater, it's much more different, coming from a place where it's just you and the ice. There are so many different variables that come into play in the game of hockey. And watching Hayden is truly an experience.

I'm sitting on the edge of my seat as I watch Hayden and Logan skate toward the player who slashed at their goalie not long ago. There are only a few minutes left in the game and the Wolves are already winning, but it looks like the two of them are definitely up to something... and I'm not sure I like it.

They approach the other player in an aggressive manner, Logan checking him and slamming him into the boards when the puck is nowhere near them. Hayden hangs back a bit, watching the scene unfold as the player gets in Logan's face. He shoves him backward as they exchange words that no one else can hear.

The two of them are suddenly throwing their gloves onto the ice as they engage in a brawl. Each of them is throwing punches, grabbing at each other's helmets and jerseys in an attempt to throw the other off the ice. I don't know how it happens, but both of their helmets end up on the ground and it's a free-for-all.

Another player from the opposing team gets involved and Hayden is quick to jump in, like this is what he was waiting for. The refs are skating toward the four guys who are openly fist fighting. My heart is in my throat as I watch Hayden try to rip the other guy's helmet off. He catches a fist to his ribs, but I'm not sure he even feels it with the way he continues to fight.

As quickly as the fight started, it's broken up,

with them all being pulled away from one another. The refs make a call, sending Logan and the first guy into the penalty box. I watch as Hayden skates back toward his bench, a smirk on his face as he glances up at me.

Hockey is a vicious sport and this is one of the things I didn't miss about it at all. I never had to worry about Chance getting into any fights because he wasn't the type to engage. Hayden, on the other hand... it's as if he and Logan went into that fight with a plan. Looking to start some kind of shit.

Both teams have power plays that last for a few minutes and then the game is over, with the Wyncote Wolves coming out on top. I can't help but feel a sense of pride as I stand up, wearing a jersey with the number 8 on the back of it and Hayden's last name. It felt weird at first because it's clear we have a connection, but I don't care anymore. Let them all think what they want.

Hayden and I know what we actually have.

As I push through the crowd and walk out of the arena, my phone vibrates in my pocket and I pause to pull it out and look at it. My gaze drops and at the same time, someone runs directly into my back, throwing me off-balance.

"Oh my goodness, I am so sorry," the girl says as I turn around to face her. Her bright blonde hair is pulled up in a high ponytail and her brown eyes meet mine.

"No, that was completely my fault," I tell her, shaking my head. "I shouldn't have stopped in the middle of the walkway here."

Her head tilts to the side slightly as her eyes scan me with what looks to be a touch of judgement. The air shifts between us and I can't quite decipher what is going on. I notice her jersey, with the opposing team's logo on it. Her gaze meets mine again and she offers me a smile.

"Have a good night," she offers as she walks past me. I can't stop my gaze from following after her, and my stomach sinks as I read the lettering along the top of her back. King, in all bold letters.

It has to just be a coincidence. I know he played for this team before, but maybe there's another player with the same last name. That's what it has to be. There's no way another girl would have one of Hayden's jerseys... especially considering his past with other girls.

———

"Hey you," Hayden breathes as he wraps his arms around me. I find him standing by one of the tables in the bar area where he told me to meet him. The entire team is here, but all of their people who came to show their support are here too. It's practically like an entire party with the amount of people occupying the area.

"Good job tonight." I smile up at him as we break apart. Hayden reaches out for me, not caring who is even around us as he slides his hand to cup the side of my face.

His smile is in his eyes. "It's because you were here and you wore this." He points at my jersey, flashing his bright white teeth at me. "That's all the luck I needed tonight."

"Well, it was quite enjoyable to watch," I tell him, shifting my weight nervously on my feet. "I'm glad you invited me to come."

Hayden stares at me for a moment. "With the way I played tonight, I might need you to come to every game."

I swallow hard over the emotion in my throat. "I think I can do that. Although, I'm not sure I like seeing you getting into fights."

The corners of his lips lift as he releases the side

of my face. "It's all in the game, baby." He chuckles, wrapping his arm around the tops of my shoulders as he pulls me over to the table. "What do you want to drink? Or eat?"

"I'll drink whatever that is," I answer him, pointing to the mixed drink he picks up from the table. "And did everyone order food already?"

Hayden shakes his head. "Just drinks. I'll go get yours from the bar so you don't have to wait. If our server comes back, just get me a cheesesteak or something."

I nod, smiling at Hayden as he disappears through the crowd. Awkwardly, I drop down into the seat next to his and pick up the menu as I wait. As I settle on a salad, the chair across from me is pulled out and I watch Sterling and Asher sit down, a smile on both of their faces.

"It's nice seeing you out like this again," Sterling says with a genuine smile and honesty in his voice. "I was wrong about you and Hayden, and I'm sorry for casting my judgement. I apologize for when I saw you at the house and the things I said. Hayden is different with you, and I can tell he's actually really into you."

I stare back at him for a moment, completely

caught off guard by his apology and admission. "I appreciate it, Sterling," I reply, offering him a smile. "I'm glad you were able to look at things differently and find it in you to apologize."

Asher chuckles. "Come on, Finley. You know Sterling. We were all friends before. Nothing any of us do or say is supposed to be malicious. We all just so happen to have a soft spot for you, even if you are a pain in the ass."

I laugh, shaking my head as his words ring in my head. "Maybe one day, if you guys get your heads out of your asses, we can be friends again."

"Are you over here hitting on my girl?" Hayden's voice breaks through our conversation as he hands me my drink and pins his gaze to Asher.

My girl.

"Get over yourself, King." Asher laughs as he takes a sip of his beer. "She was our girl before you even showed up here."

Hayden growls as he sits beside me, wrapping his arm around the top of my chair in a possessive nature. My heart is in my throat as emotions swirl through me. Picking up my drink, I take a long sip of it before turning to face Hayden.

"Calm down, not like that." I shake my head at

him, rolling my eyes. "I used to be close to these guys, but to make it clear, I was never any of their girls."

"Not like you're my girl," he murmurs, his eyes searching mine. His lips part as if he's going to say something else, but our server shows back up to take our order.

We all go around, telling her what we want before she moves on to the next group in our party. Asher and Sterling have fallen into some kind of conversation among themselves, but Hayden hasn't once taken his eyes from me. The tension hangs heavily in the air, it's tangible and energetic.

He stares at me like he's expecting some kind of a response, yet my mind can't see to form one. I need to collect myself and get my shit together. Here he is, spouting things off, and I don't know what is true or not. Am I really his girl? In the sense he's making it seem?

"I have to go to the bathroom quick, but I'll be right back," I tell him, feeling the overwhelming anxiety as I rise to my feet. My palms are sweaty and I glance back at him once more.

"Hurry back," he murmurs, the fire in his eyes burning through mine.

Swallowing hard, I nod before escaping his

penetrating gaze. I don't even need to use the restroom, but I needed some type of a getaway to try and clear my head.

At this point, I might need a cold shower instead.

CHAPTER TWENTY-SIX
HAYDEN

Way to go, Hayden.

Of course, I had to go and say something that scared her off. How stupid could I be? I didn't even give myself the chance to think before the words just came out. And once they were spoken into the universe, I wasn't taking them back. Instead, I just went with it like it was completely intentional.

Eden isn't my girl... not officially.

We've been over it enough times for each of us to make it clear that we didn't want anything more than what we had between us already. It was a lie. It was always a fucking lie. I was just too stubborn and stupid to see it at first. But now that Eden is under my skin and in my heart, I don't want her to ever leave.

I watch as she disappears through the crowd, heading toward the restrooms. The bar is packed tonight, so I don't expect her to be back right away. I'm sure there's probably a line to get in. But there's a moment as I watch her disappear that dread fills the pit of my stomach. I don't know why, but I feel like I should have gone with her. I don't want her out of my sight.

"Well, look at who decided to show his face again."

That voice. It instantly makes me cringe as I hear the sweetness laced in the venom of her tone. Glancing over my shoulder, I see Carly walking over to me. My stomach rolls as I see that she's wearing one of my old jerseys. One that she stole from my room when I was still playing here.

"Hi, Carly," I respond, keeping my voice even as she walks around to face me. Asher and Sterling have since moved on to a different table and I'm literally left with no one to interrupt this conversation.

Where the hell is Eden?

"I'm surprised to see you, especially after everything that happened," she smiles, slurring her words. She shifts her weight, stumbling slightly as some alcohol spills from the glass in her hand. I watch in slow motion as it lands on my leg, wetting my sweatpants.

"Fuck," I mumble, reaching to grab some of the napkins from the table.

"Oh my gosh." Carly giggles, spilling more of her drink as she sets it down and grabs the napkins before I can get them. "Here, let me clean up the mess I made."

I watch in horror as she starts dabbing them against my pants. This cannot be happening. I literally just want to vanish and never have to see this girl again. I knew she would be around; I just thought that maybe she would be smarter and not bother to approach me.

"I got it," I bark at her, grabbing the napkins from her as I wipe off the excess liquid. "What do you want, Carly?"

She rocks back on her heels, tipping her head to the side as her long blonde hair shifts around her shoulders. "I wore your jersey tonight, hoping I would see you," she murmurs as she places her hand on my shoulder. I thrust my arms out in an attempt to push her away, but instead I'm catching her as she falls into my lap. "I wore your old jersey, and then I saw some other girl with your new jersey on. Who is she?"

"Fuck off, Carly," I grumble, placing my hands on her hips as I go to lift her off of me. "What I do and who I do it with doesn't concern you."

"Why wasn't I enough for you, Hayden? I loved you."

Oh my god, you've got to be kidding me.

I finally get her off my lap and on her feet as I rise to my own. Tilting my head down, I meet her eyes. "It was never more than a hookup, Carly. Get the fuck over it."

Lifting my gaze, I glance around, looking for Eden, but she still isn't back. She should have been back by now. I need her to come out here. I see Sterling and Asher leaning against one of the high-top tables with their eyes on us, watching the scene as it unfolds.

"What does she have that I don't, Hayden?" Carly continues, her words slurred and thick with her plea. I don't know how the hell to handle this.

My eyes slice to hers as she reaches out and grabs my arm. "My heart."

Removing myself from her grip, I finally get away from her and shuffle over to Asher and Sterling. They're both still watching and neither of them have amused looks on their faces.

"Have either of you seen Eden?" I question them, glancing around the room again. Carly must have finally gotten the message because I don't see her where I left her.

Asher shakes his head as Sterling takes a sip of his beer. "Haven't seen her since she went to the bathroom."

"Who was that?" Sterling questions me, his gaze glued to mine.

I look between the both of them, shame washing over me. "My old coach's daughter."

"Looks like she isn't over you, King."

Swallowing roughly, I stare directly at Sterling, who is the one challenging me now. "There was never anything between us for her to get over. She's living in a fantasy—a dream world. One that will never become a reality. She was simply just a hookup, so please stop acting like we don't all do that at some point in our lives."

"And what about Eden?" he retorts, taking another sip of his beer. "You gonna leave her in the same condition as that chick?"

I shake my head. "Things with Eden are different and will never be like that."

"How are they different?"

The three of us are silent for a moment, with Asher's question hanging heavily in the air. I look between the two of them, swallowing over the emotion lodged in my throat.

"I'm in love with Eden."

CHAPTER TWENTY-SEVEN
EDEN

After finally making my way into the bathroom, I gave myself a moment to get my shit together and muster the courage to go back out to Hayden. He constantly catches me off guard and throws me off-balance. I don't know where the future is headed with him, but I think it's time we finally have an honest talk.

It's time we cut the bullshit we've been feeding each other and ourselves. At this point, we're just feeding each other lies and we're swallowing them whole like we're famished.

I don't know where this will go or how it will end up, but we can't keep playing this charade. If we keep going the way we are, it's definitely going to end badly. If we can get ahead of the heartbreak and possibly soften the blow, then that's what I want to do. I'm not sure I want to admit my feelings out loud, but I can't keep hiding them.

If Hayden King is going to call me his girl, then he needs to make me his girl. Officially.

As I push my way out of the bathroom, the line is even longer than when I first came over here. It's insane how packed the bar is, but then again, we are in a college town and it is a Saturday night. Not to mention all of the people who are here with our group.

The only thing that matters right now is getting back to Hayden... and sneaking him into my hotel room.

Walking through the bar, the air leaves my lungs as I catch sight of Hayden. He doesn't see me as my feet become cemented to the floor. I feel like I can't breathe, my throat constricting as nausea rolls in the pit of my stomach. Some girl is on Hayden's lap, in his face talking to him.

My heart sinks as I notice the jersey and remember it. It's the girl I ran into after the game—the one who had his old jersey on.

Whoever she is, she must be from Hayden's past. And with the way his hands are gripping her hips, they seem like they're well acquainted with one another. I don't know who she is and in this moment, it's irrelevant.

Whoever she is, she can fucking have him.

Usually, I wouldn't be the one who would just give in like this, but I'm waving my flag and hanging up my hat. It breaks my heart and I feel like I could vomit. It's my own fault for believing that Hayden could be different, that his reputation wasn't who he really is. I fucked up by letting him in when I knew I was going to get hurt in the end.

I just wasn't expecting this.

And I wasn't expecting it to hurt this badly.

Turning my back to the train wreck that was unfolding under my gaze, I don't bother going to any of the other guys. My eyes burn with the tears I'm trying to hold back. I can't let any of them see me fall apart again. Sterling told me to stay away from Hayden and I should have listened to him.

Hell, I should have listened to my gut instinct. I was stupid and I let Hayden get under my skin. I'm the one who let him in when I should have kept him out. I'm at a loss for thoughts and feelings right now. The emotion is taking its toll on me and I can't even decipher what I'm really feeling.

Betrayal. Hurt. Devastation. And embarrassment.

It's like everyone else knew and could see this coming, yet I was too stubborn to listen to anyone. I knew what I was getting myself into the moment I let him into my life. How could I have truly believed I wouldn't grow attached to him?

Stepping out into the night, the cold air practically slaps me across the face. Normally I would be freezing with the way the wind whips around, but I'm already numb. The cold doesn't bother me, because that's exactly what I want to feel. I want to feel the ice sliding over my heart, protecting me from the outside elements.

I walk around the building, back to where the parking lot is. It doesn't take me long to find my car. I had planned on leaving it here if I drank too much and just Ubering back to the hotel, but that isn't a concern anymore. I didn't even have a chance to be here long enough to get drunk.

As I sit down in my car, the seat is cold against my clothing. I slide the key into the ignition and twist it as I turn the engine on. The picture has been burned into my memory. Hayden sitting there with another girl on his lap, wearing his name on her back. I can't fight the tears any longer as I let my head hang. My hands grip the steering wheel, my knuckles turning white from how tight I'm holding on as sobs tear through my body.

Holding on to the steering wheel as if it's my life raft, I succumb to the sadness and the pain that lances my heart. There was a time where I would have gladly drowned in Hayden's ocean.

Now, I'm just floating. Lost and alone at sea, with nothing to anchor my soul.

After letting myself have a few moments of breaking down, I quickly gather myself together, feeling the iciness settling inside my heart. Hayden solidified why I don't let anyone get close. And I will never make the same fucking mistake again.

Pulling my car out of the lot, I leave the bar in my rearview mirror as I head down the street. My hotel is only a short drive from where we were, but I still speed there as if the car is on fire. There's a strange anxiety that is now rushing through my system. I need to get out of here and get home as soon as I can.

I can't be here, not where he is. Not after what I just saw.

It's better if I just quietly pack up my things and go. We don't have to do any kind of fighting or breaking up type of scenario. We were never together; there was never a relationship that was defined between us. We just fucked around and I caught feelings, like a goddamn idiot.

I need to put as much distance as I can between Hayden and me.

And then I can move toward forgetting this ever happened...

CHAPTER TWENTY-EIGHT
HAYDEN

I've searched every inch of this goddamn bar and I can't find Eden anywhere. I even asked some random chick to check for her in the bathroom for me, but she wasn't in there either. Panic laces itself through my veins, overriding my system. I've called her phone at least a dozen times and sent her more messages than I could count.

Every single one, she didn't even bother to leave me on read. Instead, they just showed delivered so I know she hasn't looked at a single one. I can't help but think that something bad happened to her. I wish I had a way of tracking her.

Rushing back over to the table, I find Asher and Sterling still sitting there nursing their beers. They both look at me, their eyebrows tugging together in concern.

"Neither of you have seen Eden at all?" I question them, the panic evident in my voice.

They both shake their heads. "Have you tried calling her or anything?"

"I did and she didn't answer. I don't know where the fuck she is and I'm starting to worry."

Asher purses his lips. "Maybe she went back to her hotel?"

"Why the fuck would she do that without saying something to me?" I practically snap at him. I can't help it right now. The fear is presenting itself with anger and I shouldn't take it out on either of them.

"Maybe she didn't feel well," Asher offers.

"Or maybe she saw you and that other girl," Sterling chimes in, his tone hard with accusation.

Fuck.

Closing my eyes briefly, I swallow hard, silently praying to the gods that she didn't fucking see that. It's the only reasoning I can come up with in this moment without assuming something terrible happened to her. If I were Eden, where would I go after seeing that?

"Before you jump to conclusions that something

bad happened, maybe try checking her hotel to see if she went back there for some reason?" Asher suggests, and I don't give either of them another moment of my time.

I should be thanking him for being the sound voice right now while my mind is a clusterfuck. I've already wasted enough time searching for her. If she's simply at her hotel, then I will definitely feel at ease knowing she's safe. It's at least a good place to start.

Since I came here with the team, I'm forced to take an Uber, but the closest one won't be here for twenty minutes. The hotel she's staying at is only six blocks away. Glancing up and down the street, I inhale deeply, contemplating what to do. Locking the screen on my phone, I slide it into my pocket and take off into a sprint in the direction of the building.

Fuck waiting. I don't have time to wait for an Uber to get here. I'll get there on foot a hell of a lot faster and I need to get to her *now*.

————

I'm out of breath by the time I reach the hotel building. Thankfully, I'm in shape, so it wasn't too bad of a run, but there's a reason I play hockey and don't do track. My lungs are practically screaming from the depravation of oxygen and the cold air that burned with every breath I took.

My heart pounds erratically in my chest, threatening to break free as I race to the elevator and press the button for her floor. It feels like it's an eternity, riding it up to where I might find her. I can't help but pace like a caged animal, the panic and adrenaline mixing in my system.

The elevator doors are barely open as I slide through the small opening and step out into the hall. Breaking out into a sprint, I race down to her room. I reach into my pocket, pulling out the room key I got earlier when I came in and left her my jersey and set everything up for her.

Sliding it through the key slot, it blinks green and I shove open the door in a haste. The lights are on in the suite and I hear noise coming from the bedroom. My feet move quickly as I take long strides, moving to where the sound is coming from. As I reach the door to the bedroom, my stomach sinks and my heart constricts.

Eden has her suitcase on the bed and she sniffles as she continues to shove things into the bag without bothering to fold them. I'm glad to see that she's here and safe, but fuck. My heart is in my throat at the sight of her hastily packing all of her things.

"Eden," I breathe, stepping into the room. "What are you doing? What's going on?"

She spins on her heel to look at me. Her eyes are bloodshot with streaks of mascara mixed with her tears staining her cheeks. "I'm leaving, Hayden."

"Baby, baby, baby," I murmur, stepping closer to her. My arms reach out for her, but she shakes her head and takes a step back. "No. Please, don't leave."

"I have to, Hayden. I can't do this anymore."

My heart is in my throat. "What's going on? I don't understand."

Eden tilts her head to the side, her eyes slicing to mine with an icy glare. "You don't understand? That's comical, King. I'm the one who doesn't fucking understand why you were calling me your girl and then had another one in your lap."

Fuck. She did see Carly with me.

"I promise you, it's not what it looked like at all," I implore, my voice thick with emotion. "She was drunk as shit and came over to me. I tried to get her to leave but she wouldn't."

"And what? She just so happened to fall into your lap?" Eden's frigid tone sends a shiver down my spine. She's made of ice again and I fucking hate it.

"Yes," I tell her, practically pleading. "That's exactly what happened. She tried to sit down on my lap and I tried to push her away and she lost her balance. I made her get off of me immediately."

Eden snorts and shakes her head as she turns away from me, turning back to her suitcase. "Save your bullshit for someone who will buy it, Hayden. I can't do this with you right now. Please, just leave."

"Fuck that," I growl, stepping closer to her as I pull the shirt from her hand that she was about to put into her suitcase. "I'm not fucking going anywhere until you understand that I'm telling you the truth."

Eden turns back to face me, crossing her arms defensively over her chest. "Then tell me who the hell she is and why she was wearing one of your old jerseys."

Dread rolls in the pit of my stomach. Part of me feels completely defeated. She's never going to believe me when I tell her the truth about Carly. This is over and I did exactly what Sterling told me not to do.

I fucked this up entirely.

"Her name is Carly," I admit, my voice quiet as guilt washes over me. "She's the reason why I moved to Wyncote. She was my coach's daughter and we hooked up, which caused an entire scandal. She wanted more from me and I couldn't give her that."

Eden stares at me for a moment, her face contorting as a strangled laugh slips from her plump lips. "Of course you couldn't." She sighs in defeat as tears fall from her eyes. "You have a reputation for a reason, and you know... for a moment, I believed that wasn't the real Hayden King. How fucking stupid of me."

"Eden, please listen to me," I urge, the emotion thick in my voice. "You're the only girl that I see. Since that night in your tent, it's only been you. I haven't been able to get you out of my head since. You're literally all that I want."

"Funny, considering you don't do relationships. You literally just told me about your past with this Carly chick and you expect me to believe a single word you're saying right now?"

"Yes." The word comes out in a rush. "Because I'm telling you the fucking truth. Can you stop being so fucking stubborn for two seconds and hear what I am saying? This is the truth and you told me you didn't want it."

"Well, I don't want it now either." Her words are so final, the ice sliding over her heart. "Whatever this is, is done, Hayden. I can't keep up this charade, and I'm certainly not going to look like a fool for believing you when this is over."

The tension is so thick between us, it's like I could reach out and grab it with my hands. She's hurt, completely shattered, and I don't know how to get her to believe me when I'm literally showing all my cards. She's angry, I get that, but that doesn't mean I can't be frustrated as fuck right now.

I step closer to Eden and she takes a step back. I keep inching forward and she moves farther away from her suitcase. Tearing my gaze from hers, I reach for the bag and lift it into the air.

"Put my stuff down!" Eden practically yells at me, reaching for it as I turn it over and her things begin to fall onto the floor. "What the fuck, Hayden!"

"I'm not letting you leave this hotel room until you hear everything I have to say to you."

I toss the suitcase on the bed and we're caught in an intense stare-down. Eden is closer now, only two feet away, and if I wanted, I could reach out and grab her. But I won't. I won't touch her until she wants me to. She's silent, and it's my chance to tell her the truth that I've been holding back for far too long.

"I'm in love with you, Eden Finley."

CHAPTER TWENTY-NINE
EDEN

The air leaves my lungs in a rush. I feel the color draining from my face as I stare back into his eyes. My heart clenches, my throat constricting. Part of me doesn't want to believe him, but the other part of me knows he wouldn't dare speak those words if he didn't mean them.

"I've been in love with you for longer than I wanted to admit," he tells me, his voice soft and gentle. "I thought we could keep things the way we did, but what I didn't realize was I was falling for you. And by the time I realized what was happening, it was too late. You worked your way into my heart and made yourself a home."

My breath catches in my throat that is already thick with emotion. Tears prick the corners of my eyes and I don't bother fighting them as they begin to fall down the sides of my face. His words, they reach deep inside me, tangling within the fibers of my soul. I don't know whether to hate him for this or to wrap my arms around the back of his neck and pull him to me.

"I love you, Eden Finley," he says again, stepping closer into my space until we're standing toe to toe. He slides his hand under my chin, tilting my head back to look up at him. "I've never felt this way about anyone else in my life and I know I never will. You are it for me."

A ragged breath slips from my lips and my hands shake as I lift them to cup the sides of his face. "I'm afraid to believe you," I admit, my voice barely audible. "I'm afraid of what you might do with my heart if I hand it to you."

Hayden tilts his head to the side. "I'll handle it with care, baby. I'll protect it with my fucking life. You're all that I see, Eden, and you're the only person I could imagine spending my future with." He pauses for a moment. "I want you to be my girl and I want everyone to know."

"If I dive in with you, I have terrible depth

perception. I don't know if I can survive a heartbreak from you, if we get in too deep."

A smirk plays on his lips. "We're already in deep, baby. There's no way out now, unless you want to swim to the surface. But I can promise you, I won't let you get there without me swimming after you."

Emotion consumes me, the tears falling from my eyes again. I shift my hands, wrapping my arms around the back of his neck. "I love you, Hayden. And I kind of hate you for it. I tried so hard to not let it happen, but I couldn't stop it."

"Just go with it, baby," he murmurs, sliding his hands to cup the back of my head as I look up at him. "But go with me. Tell me you'll be mine."

"Only if you tell me you're mine."

Hayden chuckles, his face dipping down to mine. "I've been yours for a long time, Eden. But, yes. This is official. We're defining this shit now. I'm going to make sure everyone knows we're together now."

"Just don't break my heart."

"Never," he breathes, his mouth colliding with mine. His lips are warm against mine, soft and gentle as we move in tandem together. Hayden spins me around, backing me up until the backs of my legs are hitting the bed.

His tongue traces the seam of my mouth and I

part my lips, letting him in. His tongue slides across mine, both caught in a torturous dance as they tangle together. I'm so lost in him, in the moment, it's as if nothing that happened before matters. We're the only thing that matters.

We both finally revealed our cards and spoke our truths into the universe. I don't know what we're really doing, but we're doing it together and that's the only thing that matters. He promises that he won't break my heart and neither of us know if that will really happen.

Life is full of risks and loving Hayden is one I'm willing to take.

He strips me of my clothes, pulling the jersey over my head and the other layers I wore underneath. Last to go is my bra before he's dropping to his knees in front of me, taking off my shoes and pants. Rising back to his feet, he wraps an arm around the back of my neck and the other around my lower back before he eases me onto the bed.

Hayden stands by the edge of the bed, his eyes filled with emotion as he stares down at me. "You're breathtaking, Eden Finley. My heart is yours to do whatever you want with it. Keep it safe or break it. I don't fucking care as long as it means I get to be loved by you."

Tears prick the corners of my eyes as he begins to strip himself of his own clothes, leaving them in a pile on the floor with mine. I scoot back on the bed and he lowers himself down on his knees. Crawling toward me, he doesn't stop until he's hovering above me, settling between my legs.

Parting my thighs wider, I give him full access. His mouth drops down to mine as his cock presses against my pussy. Shifting my hips, I lift up as he slowly eases into me. There's a small amount of friction as he slides in, but it quickly dissipates as I get wetter just from his touch. He stretches me wide and I moan into his mouth as he shifts his hips, slowly moving in and out.

There's a shift between us. Before, there would have been more urgency. Instead, this is fueled purely by emotion. By love. And I'll let him love me for an eternity if it feels like this with him. This side of Hayden—I'm obsessed. And this part of him is mine and mine only. Something he's never shared with anyone else.

We're lost in each other, lost in the moment, as he continues to thrust his hips. His cock strokes my insides and I lift my legs, wrapping them around his waist. Pulling him closer to me, he slides his hand down to cup my ass as he lifts it into the air. It allows him deeper access and he fills me to the brim with one thrust.

Hayden moves his mouth from mine, trailing his lips up and down the side of my neck. He tastes and teases my skin as he continues to fuck me. Each thrust is harder than the one before and he's driving both of us closer to the brink of ecstasy.

His lips brush the outer shell of my ear. "Come for me, baby," he murmurs, nipping at my lobe. "I want to feel you come all over my cock."

His words are all that I need to feel myself nearing the edge. One simple demand and the warmth is spreading through my body like rapid fire. I feel it in the pit of my stomach as my pussy clenches around him. He thrusts once more and my orgasm tears through my body like a hurricane. I'm a mess, moaning his name as I come completely undone around him.

"That's it, Eden," he groans as his thrusts become harder. "I love the way your pussy feels, clenching me like a vise grip as you lose yourself."

"Come with me," I breathe, completely in a daze as pleasure continues to flow through my system.

Hayden thrusts again, spilling himself inside me as he reaches his peak. We're falling into the abyss, wrapped up in one another with our souls tangled together. He slowly pulls out of me, both of us riding out our highs. My head is soaring through the clouds and I notice him abandon the bed in a daze.

He's only gone for a short amount of time before he's walking back into the room with a warm wash-cloth. Kneeling between my legs, he cleans me up before tossing the cloth onto the floor. Crawling up the bed, he falls onto his side and pulls me close to him until my back is flush against his chest.

His arm is warm and I feel at home as he wraps it around me, holding me to him tightly. "I love you, Eden. And you better get used to hearing me tell you that over and over again."

A smile tugs on the corners of my lips. "I'll never get tired of hearing it."

"Good." I hear the smile in his voice as he presses his lips to the back of my neck. "Because I'm going to tell you that every chance I get."

"Don't stop."

"I'm never going to stop, baby. What we have is a forever love, and I'm going to make sure you never go a moment of your life not feeling the love that I have for you."

Relaxing in his arms, I settle against Hayden.

The guy I've loved longer than I was willing to admit. The one who holds my heart in his hands, and I hope to God he never lets it go.

My Hayden.

EPILOGUE
HAYDEN

SIX MONTHS LATER

I watch in awe as Eden skates backward, her entire body lifting into the air as she spirals. I barely pay attention to how many spins it actually is before her skate is landing on the ice with her other leg out behind her. She makes it look so flawless, but there's something captivating and artistic about the way she moves.

I love Eden when she's in her element like this. Completely lost in what she's doing. It's amazing how she can immerse herself in the entire experience and truly experience it. Her performance is just as amazing as the first time I watched her skate.

And sitting here, watching her compete for the

championship, I can't help but feel a swell of pride in my chest. She's been working her ass off, putting in so many hours to perfect her performance. It's not an easy task either. All it takes is one move that isn't the exact way it should be and you're having points deducted.

Not to mention the constant threat of falling. Even though there's so much time and practice put into figure skating, it doesn't take much to have you landing on your ass. A simple misstep or your skate not landing correctly can easily make you fall.

Take it from someone else who practically spends their life on the ice. Even though I'm not springing myself into the air and spinning around like Eden, I know how easily you can end up falling. Although, it's a little more acceptable in hockey. It won't cause you to lose a game, like it could jeopardize an entire figure skating competition.

Eden skates back to the center of the rink as she finishes up her performance. With one skate behind her, she slides her leg down as she bends her other knee. She ends her performance with perfection and you can feel the confidence radiating from the arena as she bows her head.

I'm on my feet before the rest of the crowd and soon everyone is clapping for her. Eden rises up, her smile broad and her eyes shining. I'm a few rows off the ice, but from here, I can still see that she knows she fucking nailed it. Eden turns to both sides of the audience, bowing to them before she skates off to where her coach and teammates are.

After a few moments, the judges come forward with their score and the announcer informs the crowd that Eden is now in first place. And her score is practically untouchable. My throat constricts with emotion and my heart triples in size. I know how much work Eden has put in to get to this point and I know how important this day is for her.

Winning this championship just puts her one step closer to the Winter Olympics.

There are two more skaters left, but I'm not here for either of them. Rising from my seat, I slip out of the row and head down to where the competitors are. A guard stops me as I reach the last doorway, prohibiting me from coming through.

"I'm just trying to see my girlfriend," I explain, motioning to where she's standing with her coach. "I had a hockey game, so I wasn't able to get a badge from her this morning to come back here."

"I'm sorry, man," the guys says, frowning. "I can't let you through without clearance. I'm sure you understand."

"Hayden!" I hear Eden's voice as she calls out my name. She jogs over to me with her skate guards on, covering the blades. Her short dress sways around her thighs and I'm at a loss for words at her beauty. "He's with me," she tells the guard as she shows him a badge.

The man looks at it and nods before stepping out of the way. Eden stares at me for a moment, her eyes shining brightly before she practically squeals and throws herself into my arms.

"Oh my god, Hayden," she breathes, a soft laugh falling from her lips. "I'm so glad you're here."

A chuckle vibrates in my chest. "There's nowhere else I would rather be, baby."

Eden releases my neck and takes a step back. Her hand is cold as she slips it into mine, our fingers lacing together as she leads me back to her little group. Her coach nods at me and the girls that I recognize all say hi. They've all seen a lot of me the past few months since Eden and I started officially dating.

I'm literally obsessed with her, sometimes I'm afraid it's unhealthy. Even though we have our own things to occupy our time, I still can't get enough of her. I need her around me all the time.

Who would have thought that the university's playboy would become a stage five clinger?

"You looked so good out there, Eden," I tell her as I pull her toward me. She lifts onto her toes, pressing her lips to mine before landing back on flat skates. "All of your hard work paid off."

"Eden," Winter whisper-yells at her. "The other skaters are done and they're getting ready to announce who won."

"Oh my god, okay." Eden nods at her, swallowing hard over her nerves. She turns around in my arms with them still linked around her waist as she looks out at the ice rink. "I feel like my stomach is going to roll out of my body right now."

"You did amazing, Eden," I breathe, burying my face in the crook of her neck. "You blew their scores out of the water."

"That doesn't mean anything," she argues, refusing to get her hopes up. "Things constantly change and I refuse to believe it until I know for sure."

It feels like time is suspended as we wait to hear the judges. After what feels like an eternity, the announcer's voice comes back through the speaker. He announces the first place winner and it's Eden.

That's my fucking girl.

I hear her breath catch in her throat as she spins on her skates to face me again. Looping her arms around the back of my neck, her eyes are filled with tears as they bounce back and forth between mine. "They said my name, Hayden. Winning this means I get to go to the qualifying competition for the Olympics."

"I heard him, baby. You fucking did it."

My face drops down to hers, capturing her lips with mine in a swift kiss. I release her as quickly as I kissed her, urging her away from me. "You better get out there before they give your medal to someone else," I tell her.

The lilt of Eden's laughter is like music to my ears. She jogs over to the door that leads into the rink and pulls off her skate guards before stepping out onto the ice. I walk toward the boards, stopping beside Winter as we both watch Eden skate into the middle of the arena.

"You better wife her up, King," Winter says, smiling as we watch the judges hand Eden a bouquet of flowers and place her medal around her neck. I know it's tradition to bring someone flowers when they perform, but I have something better.

I look over at Winter. "Oh, I plan on it."

The judges announce second and third place and

both skaters head out into the center of the rink, one of them being Winter. I stand by the door, watching my girl as she does a skate around the perimeter of the rink, and my heart crawls into my throat.

We've come a long fucking way and sometimes, it still feels like this is all a dream. Sometimes I have to remind myself that this is our reality now. That she's really mine.

The three skaters all head back to the middle of the rink, all bowing one last time before heading off the ice. As Eden gets closer to us, the announcer asks her to come back to the center of the rink, and I know that's my cue.

Breaking into a sprint, I slip through the door where the guard is, telling him I'll be right back. I run as fast as I can, stopping where I hid my spare pair of skates in an unlocked closet I found. Grabbing them, I race back to where Eden's coach and teammates are standing.

Winter tilts her head to the side, watching me as I lace up my skates quicker than I ever have before. "What the hell are you doing, Hayden?" she questions me, her eyebrows pulling together. "You can't go out there."

I had this all set up two nights ago. It took a lot of sweet talking and convincing to do... not to mention a little bit of money. But I got it accomplished and was able to get the officials on my side.

Eden's eyes meet mine as I step out onto the ice and begin to skate toward her. A wave of confusion passes through her expression and she truly looks concerned. She starts to move in my direction and I push off harder, using the muscles in my legs to reach her while she's still close to the center of the rink.

"Hayden," she whispers, glancing around before looking back at me with concern. "You're not allowed out here. You're going to get us both in trouble."

She tips her beautiful face back to look up at me, and I smile. I'm so gone and lost in her, words could never describe how much I love her. Taking both of her hands in mine, she continues to stare at me in confusion, but she doesn't question me as she awaits for some type of response from me.

As I drop down onto one knee, releasing her hands as I reach into the front pocket of my jeans, I watch her face transform. Emotion swirls in her gold irises, and she brings both of her hands to her mouth as she lets out a gasp. Tears fill those beautiful eyes and I smile up at her as I hold out a small velvet box.

"I love you, Eden Finley, with every fiber of my being. I gave you my heart, when really you already took my soul. You worked your way into my heart and I never had a chance of stopping it. And even if I could have, I would never have wanted to. When I look at my future, all I can see is you. I want you to be my wife, to one day start a family together. You're the only person I want to continue this journey with."

Eden stares down at me, tears streaming down her cheeks as she slowly pulls her hands away from her face. "Oh my god, Hayden," she breathes, her voice shaking. "You're absolutely insane."

"Insane about you, baby." I smile up at her. "Will you marry me and make me the goddamn happiest man in the world?"

"Yes." She nods, a strangled laugh slipping from her lips. "Of course I will marry you."

Flipping open the box, she gasps as she sees the perfectly cut diamond that I had handpicked for her. Plucking the ring from it, I fold the velvet box and slip it back into my pocket before taking her left hand. We both watch, completely transfixed as I slide the ring onto her finger.

As I rise back to my feet, Eden throws her arms around the back of my neck, pulling herself flush against my body as she buries her face in my chest. The entire arena goes insane, the crowd clapping and cheering for us. Eden pulls away, her tear-filled eyes searching mine.

"You're sneaky." She laughs softly, shaking her head in disbelief. "You had this whole thing planned, didn't you? What would you have done if I didn't win?"

Dropping my face to hers, I nip at her bottom lip. "I knew you would win, Eden. We both play to win and right now, I think we're tied."

"I don't know," she breathes, her lips brushing against mine. "I think you might have just one-upped me. I need to come up with a better surprise than this, but I don't think I can outdo this one."

"So, I did good then?"

"You always do," she murmurs as our lips connect, melting together.

Our surroundings fade away and no one in this entire arena matters except for the two of us. We're lost in each other, in this moment that will forever be ingrained in my mind. Eden Finley is my entire world, and now she's going to be my wife.

To have and to hold for the rest of my life.

HAYDEN AND EDEN BONUS SCENE

HAYDEN

Eden's hand fits perfectly in mine as we walk through the resort, palm trees hanging above our heads. We got to Barbados last night and have a full two weeks that we're here. She tried to argue that it was too long to spend away, but there was no way in hell we were only doing a week here.

I wanted to treat my wife to the best honeymoon I could give her. And I don't even know whether this is the best I could have done, but this is where she decided she wanted to come. My plan is to take her somewhere special and different every year for our anniversary.

It will almost be like an annual honeymoon,

where we can do this all over again and act like we're newlyweds.

Although, I don't think either of us have to worry about the honeymoon phase of our relationship ever dissipating. We've been together long enough now and I'm still as fucking obsessed with her as I was in the beginning.

Eden was the mystery I wanted to unravel, and she finally granted me that wish.

Now, she's my fucking wife. It still seems surreal, even though our wedding was literally two days ago. I want to go back in time and live that day over again, just because of how amazing it was. We were surrounded by our family and friends that day. Eden floated down the aisle like a goddamn goddess.

It's a memory I will never be able to get out of my head and thank fuck for that. If it was acceptable, I would make her wear that damned wedding dress every day. Although, seeing Eden in her bikini right now is a whole different experience.

Only I know what's beneath the small pieces of material that cover her skin.

We reach the pool area and there isn't anyone around, thankfully. I don't know where all the guests are, but we chose a smaller resort for this purpose. We wanted as much alone time as possible. Eden dips her toe into the hot tub before sinking down into the water until it reaches her chin.

I follow in after her, feeling the heat as I submerge my body in it. Eden positions herself with her back against one of the jets. Her arms are stretched out behind her on the concrete, and she tips her head back

"This feels so good," she sighs, lifting her head to meet my gaze. "I love it here."

A chuckle rumbles in my chest as I make my way over to her, sitting on the bench beside her. "We just got here, baby. And I've got plans for us while we're here."

She tilts her head to the side. "Oh yeah? Like different excursions?"

I shrug, a smirk pulling on my lips as I grab her hips and pull her onto my lap. "You'll just have to wait and see."

She shakes her head in defiance. "No, tell me. What are your plans for us?"

"Well," I murmur, dipping my head into the crook of her neck as I place my lips to her skin. "Since you really want to know... how about I show you what one of them is?"

Eden places her hands on my shoulders, her

nails digging into my flesh as I trail my lips along her neck. I drag my tongue along the column of her throat, tasting the saltiness from the ocean on her skin. I feel her moan vibrate through her body as she shifts her hips on my lap, grinding against my erection in my swim trunks.

My hands leave her hips for a moment as I reach down between us. I slide my fingers along her pussy, feeling her warmth through the bottom of her bathing suit. "Mmm," I groan against her skin, my cock throbbing.

"What are you doing, Hayden?" she breathes, her voice hoarse with need. "We can't do this here."

"Says who?" I pull back, looking into her bright, golden eyes. "No one's around and if I want to fuck my wife in the hot tub, I dare them to try and fucking stop me."

She gasps as I slip my finger under her bathing suit bottom, sliding directly into her tight pussy. She's fucking wet as hell already and that's exactly how I want her. Writhing under my touch as I fuck her senseless.

"Take them off," she half moans, her eyes fluttering as she stares at me.

I shake my head. "I'm going to fuck you with them on."

Pulling my finger from her, I grab the waistband of my swim trunks and pull them down. They aren't off, but they're down enough to get my cock out. Hooking my finger under the bottom of her bathing suit, I push it to the side as I guide her against me.

The tip presses into her and she lowers herself as she takes in my entire length. A moan falls from her lips as she sits on my lap, her nails still digging into my flesh. "Goddamn," she breathes, her eyes filled with a fire as she looks at me.

Grabbing her hips, I lift her up and down, stroking her insides with my cock. Eden shifts her hips, bouncing up and down on me as we get lost in the moment. Someone could easily see us, but neither of us care. The water in the hot tub splashes around, spilling out over the edges as I continue to top her from the bottom, fucking her harder.

I fill her to the brim, my cock hitting all the right places inside of her. She grinds herself against me, the close proximity causing friction against her clit. My fingertips grip her ass as I continue to pound into her, fucking her with no hesitation.

I literally dare someone to try and stop us right now.

Eden is out of breath as she continues to move against me, her pussy clenching around me. She's getting closer to the edge and I'm ready to push her off. For both of us to free fall into the euphoria we bring each other to.

"Come for me, Eden," I demand, fucking her harder. "Your pussy is so wet right now. I want to feel you lose yourself all over me."

Her nails are sharp in my flesh, her head tipping back as she lets her body take over. She's nearing closer to her orgasm and I feel my balls beginning to draw closer to my body as I broach my own. We're so close—so fucking close right now.

Our surroundings fade and the only thing that matters right now is Eden. She's the most important thing to me. Fuck the rest.

"Oh god," she cries out, her inhibitions gone as she doesn't care if anyone hears her. "Don't stop, Hayden."

Slamming into her once more, that's all it takes before I send her plummeting over the edge. Her orgasm tears through her body like a hurricane, her legs shaking as her pussy grips the fuck out of my cock. I thrust into her, feeling the heat spread through my body like wildfire as my own orgasm consumes my body.

I'm deep inside her, filling her with my cum as we continue to fuck, our movements slowing as we're lost in a state of ecstasy. We're both out of breath and Eden straightens her head, her eyes glazed over like she's drunk as she looks at me.

"You have more plans of this while we're here?" she breathes, still in my lap with her hands on my shoulders.

A smirk tugs on the corners of my lips. "I plan on fucking my wife all over this goddamn resort."

"I like the sound of that." She smiles back at me.

"You fucking better."

I have yet to have my fill of Eden and I doubt I ever will. I'm ready for forever with this beautiful woman in my lap, but for now, I'm going to savor every moment as we're living them. Eden Finley stole my heart.

And now Eden King completely owns it.

NEXT IN THE SERIES

The Goalie Who Stole Christmas is the fifth book from the Wyncote Wolves, featuring Asher and Sydney. Continue reading on the next page for a look inside The Goalie Who Stole Christmas.

THE GOALIE WHO STOLE CHRISTMAS

Prologue

Asher

Of course, this is the exact situation I should have expected to find myself in. Even though I'm the middle child, I always expected that I would be the last one of my siblings to get married. I never quite fit in with the way they live their lives and I've always been a little different than the rest of them. My mother always seemed too accepting of it, but over the past few years, she's really put on the pressure for me to settle down with someone.

I know she knows how important hockey is and how that will always come first. I also know that after her breast cancer diagnosis last year, she has wanted to speed up everything in her children's lives. I'm sure there's a weird sense of being reminded of her mortality.

Thankfully, she was able to have a double mastectomy and undergo chemotherapy in an effort to stop any other possible cancer cells in her body. The doctors are hoping that she is in remission, but there's a part of her that doesn't think she's going to make it out alive. And that has been the reason why she's pushing so hard for everyone to speed things up in their lives.

Even though she's only in her fifties, she's terrified she won't see all of her children get married. She won't get to see her grandchildren. My mother knows how I am; she knows I don't seriously date anyone. I may have in high school, but that didn't really count. Now, she's been pushing so hard and constantly questioning me on why I'm still single.

I've tried to ignore her, but she just won't let it go. Literally over the past year, since she was diagnosed, my two older sisters got married, and now my little brother is getting married later this month. Which leaves me as the one who gets to be the disappointment. The one kid who doesn't have anyone, who would rather be alone and just focus on the life I'm trying to build around hockey.

My parents were supportive—they still are—but my mother wants me to experience other things in life. Even though by going to the professional league I will be set for the rest of my life, none of that matters. And that's easy for her to say. She and my father have already built a life together, so she doesn't have to worry about how she will pay the bills or take care of herself.

And there's a part of her that doesn't want me to worry about that either, but I'm not going to rely on my parents. Not at twenty-one years old. I haven't lived with them in almost three years, I'm not going back to that life now.

I barely even pay attention during any of my classes today, because my brain is so focused on the messages my mother sent me this morning. She's asking if I'm bringing a plus-one to the wedding. And the truth is, no... I don't have a date. I didn't have any plans of finding one, but now the pressure is on.

The last thing I want to do is disappoint my mother.

So, it looks like I'm finding a fake girlfriend to take to my brother's wedding.

ALSO BY CALI MELLE

ABOUT THE AUTHOR

Cali Melle is a contemporary romance author who loves writing stories that will pull at your heart-strings. You can always expect her stories to come fully equipped with heartthrobs and a happy ending, along with some steamy scenes and some sports action. In her free time, Cali can usually be found spending time with her family or with her nose in a book. As a hockey and figure skating mom, you can probably find her freezing at a rink while watching her kids chase their dreams.

Printed in the USA
CPSIA information can be obtained
at www.ICGtesting.com
LVHW041231041023
760010LV00004B/560

9 781960 963017